# LITTLE WOMEN

# LITTLE WOMEN

Louisa May Alcott

*Foreword by*

Ruskin Bond

RUPA

Published by
Rupa Publications India Pvt. Ltd 2018
161-B/4, Gulmohar House,
Yusuf Sarai Community Centre,
New Delhi 110049

*Sales centres:*
Bengaluru Chennai
Hyderabad Kolkata Mumbai



P-ISBN: 978-81-291-2401-2
E-ISBN: 978-93-5304-122-9

Fourteenth impression 2025

20 19 18 17 16 15 14

Printed in India

# CONTENTS

# FOREWORD

Drama and eccentricity are at the root of every close-knit family's bond. Indian families, though, are at the very forefront of it. In the early 1960s, when new colonies were still settling in Delhi post the independence—in the area of Rajouri Garden, there lived a lively Punjabi middle-class family with whom I nearly always stayed when I was in Delhi. In the small house, there was Bhabhiji—Granny—the head of the family who had complete control over her large household and, with tremendous confidence and enthusiasm, presided over the lives of her three sons, a daughter, two daughters-in-law and fourteen grandchildren. Even when her husband had been alive, Bhabhiji had dominated the family. The underlying tensions had always been obvious in that house, yet there was love, commitment and unity among them, which kept the family above everything.

And so it is world over, not just India. Family is what sticks by you always, in times of sorrow and in times of happiness. I read somewhere that Louisa May Alcott loosely based *Little Women* on her own life and her three sisters; you see, inspiration too comes from those closest to you.

This is a widely popular children's fiction that will take the reader through the passage from childhood to womanhood of the March sisters—Meg, Jo, Beth and Amy.

I would suggest that you do not mistake this classic novel

for one on the themes of domesticity and femininity. For, it is much beyond that—its colourful characters reflect a social and familial reality, and draw you in with their vulnerability. The moral lessons and the historical significance apart, these little women will charm you with their innocence and wistful insights.

So, sit back, enjoy this bestselling novel, and lose yourself in its old-world charm while you snuggle warmly in bed with a cup of tea.

**Ruskin Bond**

# INTRODUCTION

Without a doubt, *Little Women* is Louisa May Alcott's best-known work. It is an enduring classic following the lives of the spirited March sisters. The book traces the sisters' contrasting personalities and fortunes over a period of fifteen years—from childhood to becoming adults—and their encounters with the struggles posed by employment, societal norms and marriage.

The story's charm and innocence continues to engage readers even today, despite the fact that the family structure depicted in the book is very different from a contemporary domestic life. Jo March is one of the most loved characters in children's literature. In fact, children, both boys and girls, can identify with her. Though, in the present day, the March girls seem too good, but in Alcott's society, the girls were considered flawed as they were selfish, vane, given to temper and bashful.

Alcott wrote *Little Women* to earn money. What she never imagined, however, was that it would enchant readers generation after generation and become a classic of children's fiction. It is often said that the appeal of the book lies in the fact that everyone can identify with at least one character from among this American household, even if it is a minor character.

## NOTE ON THE AUTHOR

**Louisa May Alcott** was born on 29 November 1832 in Germantown, Pennsylvania, USA. Alcott is best known for her children's books, especially *Little Women.*

She spent most of her life in Boston and Concord, Massachusetts, where she often met Ralph Waldo Emerson, Theodore Parker and Henry David Thoreau. Her education was largely under the direction of her father both, at his school and at home. Alcott learnt early that her father was impractical and when his utopian community—called Fruitlands—failed, she took upon her the charge of the family. She worked as a teacher and a domestic help before turning to writing.

Alcott's initial works were thrillers but her latter works portrayed strong and self-reliant women. She volunteered and worked briefly as a nurse during the American Civil War but when her health declined, she was sent home. She was never able to regain her health completely. In 1863, she compiled and published her letters, *Hospital Sketches,* about her experiences during the war. These brought her the first taste of fame.

Alcott's stories began to appear in *The Atlantic Monthly,* between 1868 and 1869, she wrote the autobiographical *Little Women,* which was a tremendous success. Based on her recollections of her own childhood, *Little Women* describes the domestic adventures of the Marches, a family of modest means but optimistic outlook. *Little Women* created a realistic picture of family life with which her readers could easily identify. She followed *Little Women*'s success by writing *An Old-Fashioned Girl* (1870); *Aunt Jo's Scrap Bag*, 6 vol. (1872–82); *Little Men* (1871); *Eight Cousins* (1875); *Rose in Bloom* (1876); and *Jo's Boys* (1886).

She spent most of her life in Boston and Concord, caring for her ill mother and helpless father. Her own health too declined, and she died in Boston days after her father's death.

Alcott's books for younger readers have remained steadfastly popular. *A Modern Mephistopheles*, published pseudonymously in 1877 and republished in 1987, is a Gothic novel about a failed poet who makes a Faustian bargain. *Work: A Story of Experience* (1873), is based on Alcott's own struggles and tells the story of a poor girl trying to support herself by doing menial jobs are some of her works that have been republished in recent times.

# CHARACTERS IN FOCUS

### Josephine March

She is the protagonist of the novel and the second-oldest March sister. Jo wants to be a writer. She has quite a temper and a quick tongue, though she tries to control both. A tomboy, she is an advocate for women's rights and has no interest in romance. Her only ambition is to keep her family together.

### Meg March

She is the oldest March sister. She is responsible, kind and loving, though she likes to indulge in little luxuries. She represents the conventional and the good and tries to please others. Meg falls in love with John Brooke, a poor tutor, and marries him. She forgoes her indulgence in luxury and becomes an agreeable wife.

### Beth March

Beth is the third March sister. She is quiet, virtuous, shy and always makes an effort to please others. She loves to play the piano. Just like Jo, she makes efforts to keep the family together.

### Amy March

She is the youngest March sister. She is an artist and is a little vane. She has a weakness for pretty possessions and has a temper. She is good at manipulating people and often pretends to be a lady to please others. She marries Laurie, the rich boy living next door.

### Laurie Laurence

Theodore Laurence, lovingly called 'Laurie' or 'Teddy' is rich and friendly. He is considered family in the March household. Laurie is charming, clever, intelligent and good at heart. He struggles with his grandfather's expectations of him who wants Laurie to continue their family business. He is close to Jo though he marries Amy.

# OTHERS YOU WILL MEET

### Marmee or Mrs March

She is the March girls' mother. Marmee is a role model for her daughters. She counsels them whenever they have a problem. She works hard to make a living while her husband is away at war. She is happy and content with her life and surroundings.

### Mr March

He is the March sisters' father and husband to Marmee. He serves in the army as a chaplain and is away from home. When he returns, he begins practising as a minister in a nearby parish.

### Mr Brooke

He is Laurie's tutor. Mr Brooke is poor but virtuous. He marries Meg.

### Frederick Bhaer

He is a respected professor in Germany and a language instructor in America. He is kind. Mr Bhaer lives in New York, where he meets Jo.

### Mr Laurence

He is Laurie's grandfather. He is kind and loving though he seems gruff. He treats Beth as his own granddaughter.

### Aunt March

She is the March girls' aunt and a rich widow. She is a difficult person but she adores her nieces and wants the best for them.

### The Hummels

They are a poor family living near the Marches house. The family has half-a-dozen sickly children. Often, the Marches help them and nurse the sickly to health.

# Part I

## Chapter 1

'Christmas won't be Christmas without any presents,' grumbled Jo, lying on the rug.

'Isn't it dreadful to be poor?' sighed Meg, looking at her old dress.

'It's not fair for some girls to have plenty of good things and other girls to have nothing at all,' added little Amy, with a sniff.

'We've got Father, Mother and each other,' said Beth with genuine contentment.

The four young faces on which the firelight shone, brightened at the cheerful words, but darkened again as Jo said sadly, 'We haven't got Father and shall not have him for a long time.'

Each girl became quiet and sad, as they thought of Father on the warfront. All were quiet for a minute; then Meg said, 'You know why Mother proposed not having any presents this Christmas? It's going to be a hard winter for everyone and so we ought not to spend money for pleasure, when our men are suffering so for our sake.'

'I don't think the little we would spend would make any difference. We've each got just a dollar, and the army wouldn't be much helped by that,' added Amy.

The four sisters, sat knitting away in the twilight, while the December snow fell quietly outside and the fire crackled cheerfully within. It was a comfortable room, though the carpet was faded and the furniture very plain.

Margaret, the eldest of the four, was sixteen. She was pretty, with large eyes, plenty of soft brown hair, a sweet mouth and white hands. Fifteen-year-old Jo was very tall, thin and brown. She had a determined mouth and sharp, grey, thoughtful eyes. Her long, thick hair was her one beauty, which she usually bundled into a net, to be kept out of her way. Jo had the uncomfortable appearance of a girl who was rapidly shooting up into a woman and didn't like it. Elizabeth or Beth, as everyone called her, was a rosy, smooth-haired, bright-eyed girl of thirteen, shy, with a peaceful expression which was seldom disturbed.

Amy, the youngest, was a regular snow maiden, with blue eyes, yellow hair curling on her shoulders, pale and slender, who always carried herself like a young lady, mindful of her manners. The clock struck six. Mother was about to arrive and everyone brightened to welcome her. Meg got up and lighted the lamp.

'Let's each of us get her something for Christmas and not get anything for ourselves,' said Beth.

The girls, then, decided to surprise Marmee on Christmas night.

'I am glad to find you so cheerful, my girls,' said a elated voice at the door and the girls turned to welcome their mother.

'Well, my dears, how was your day?' Marmee enquired as she sat down, ready to enjoy the happiest hour of her day. Then, with a particularly happy face, she added, 'I've got a treat for you all!'

A quick, bright smile went round like a streak of sunshine as they exclaimed, 'A letter from Father!'

'Yes, a nice long one. He is well. He sends his best wishes for Christmas and an especial message to you girls,' said Mrs March, patting her pocket.

'How I wish I could be near him and help him,' exclaimed Jo, with a sigh.

They all drew close to the fireplace. Mother sat in the big chair with the girls around her. It was a cheerful letter, full of lively descriptions of camp life and military news; only at the end did the writer's heart overflow with fatherly love and longing for the little girls at home.

'Give them all my love. Tell them I think of them by day, pray for them by night. I know they will be loving children to you, do their duty so beautifully that when I come back to them I may be fonder and prouder than ever before, of my little women.'

Everybody sniffed when they came to that part. Mrs March broke the silence that followed saying, 'Do you remember how you used to play *Pilgrim's Progress* when you were little babies?'

'Let us do it,' said Meg. 'It is an interesting way for trying to be good. Though we do want to be good, it's difficult and we forget.'

'Look under your pillows on Christmas morning for your guidebook,' replied Mrs March.

They sang, as usual, before they went to bed. No one but Beth could get music out of the old piano. Meg had a voice like a flute; she and mother led the choir. Amy chirped like a cricket. Jo would join in at her own sweet will at the wrong place with a croak that spoiled the most pensive tune. They had always done this from the time they could lisp and it had become a household custom, for mother was a born singer.

## Chapter Highlights

- The four March sisters—Margaret, Jo, Elizabeth and Amy—are sitting in their comfortable living room lamenting about their poverty. In time, their thoughts turn to their father who is serving in the army. They become sad realizing that he will not be with them on Christmas.
- The sisters decide to surprise their mother, whom the girls call Marmee, on Christmas by buying her a present.
- Just then, their mother arrives and says that she has a surprise for the girls. One of the girls cry out saying that it is a letter from their father.
- As Marmee settles down near the fireplace, the four girls gather around her and listen to their mother read the letter. Their father misses them and longs to see his daughters.
- Later, the girls decide to enact *Pilgrim's Progress*, something they used to do when they were younger. Soon, the girls are cheerful as Beth plays the piano and the others sing to its tunes.

## Chapter 2

Jo was the first to wake in the grey dawn of Christmas morning. Finding no stockings hanging at the fireplace, she was disappointed but soon she remembered her mother's promise.

Slipping her hand under her pillow, she drew out a little crimson-covered book. She knew it very well, for it was that beautiful old story of the best life ever lived and Jo felt that it was a true guidebook for any pilgrim going on a long journey. She woke Meg with a 'Merry Christmas' and asked her to look under her pillow. Soon the four girls found their books with a few words written by their mother, which made their presents more precious to them.

'Girls,' said Meg seriously, 'Mother wants us to read these books and follow the morals. We must begin at once. We used to be faithful about it; but since Father went away and the war has unsettled us, we have neglected many things.'

While the pages were softly being turned, the winter sunshine crept in to touch the bright heads and serious faces with a Christmas greeting.

'Where is Mother, Hannah?' asked Meg, as she and Jo ran down to wish her.

'Some poor creeter came a-beggin', and your ma went straight off to see what was needed. There never was such a woman for helping,' replied Hannah, who was treated more as a friend than a servant.

'She will be back soon, so keep everything ready,' said Meg, looking over the presents which were collected in a basket and kept under the sofa, ready to be produced at the proper time.

'There's Mother. Hide the basket, quickly!' cried Jo, as they heard the door open.

Amy who had been missing, came in hastily, looking uncomfortable when she saw her sisters waiting for her.

Another bang of the entrance door sent the basket under the sofa and the girls to the table, eager for breakfast.

'Merry Christmas, Marmee! Thank you for our books. We read some and mean to read every day,' they all cried in chorus.

'Merry Christmas, my lovely little daughters! I'm glad you began reading at once and hope you will keep on. I want to tell you all something before we sit down for breakfast. Not far away from here, stays a poor woman with a little newborn baby. Six children are huddled into one bed to save themselves from freezing, for they have no fire. They have nothing to eat! My girls, will you give them your breakfast as a Christmas present?'

They were all unusually hungry. No one spoke for a minute and then Jo exclaimed, 'I'm so glad you came before we began!'

'I knew you'd all agree,' said Mrs March, beaming with satisfaction. 'We shall all go and when we return, we will have bread and milk for breakfast and make it up at dinnertime.'

And it was done likewise. The girls had a very happy breakfast, though they didn't get any of it. As they returned, leaving comfort behind, the hungry little girls contented themselves with bread and milk on Christmas morning and yet they were the happiest four people in the entire city.

'Be ready, Beth! Three cheers for Marmee!' cried Jo, prancing about as Meg escorted her with great dignity. Mrs March was both surprised and touched. She smiled with her eyes full of tears as she examined her presents and read the little notes which accompanied them.

On Christmas evening, a dozen girls, all friends from the neighbourhood, piled onto the bed—which was the dress circle for the show at the Marches and sat in a state of expectancy for the curtains to draw. The curtains flew apart and the drama began. Tumultuous applause followed the five-act play, full of melodrama and some moments of hilarity but it came to an abrupt halt, for the folding cot suddenly closed along with the enthusiastic audience. All were unhurt but speechless with laughter. The excitement had hardly appeased, when Mrs March requested the ladies to walk down to supper.

When they saw the table, they looked at each other in rapturous amazement. It was expected from Marmee to surprise them with a little treat but anything so fine and elaborate was unheard of. They stared first at the table and then at their mother, who looked as if she enjoyed it immensely.

Old Mr Laurence had arranged to treat the children as Hannah had told one of his servants about the morning with Hummels which pleased him. Mother told the girls that he knew her father years ago. He had sent her a polite note, asking if he could express his affection for the children by sending them a few trifles. She could not refuse and therefore the feast.

## Chapter Highlights

- It is Christmas morning. Jo is the first to wake up. Looking under her pillow, she sees a crimson-covered little book. The others girl too find copies of the same book. The girls are happy and soon are reading their copy of the book.
- After a while, Meg makes inquiries about their mother from their servant Hannah. They learn that someone had come to get some help and that Marmee has gone with the person to see what was needed.
- Then, the girls hide the presents for their mother in a basket under the sofa. When Marmee comes back, the breakfast table is laid and the girls thank their mother for the books.
- Marmee informs them that a poor and hungry family, the Hummels, lives nearby. She asks the girls if they will give their breakfast as Christmas present to the family. The girls give their breakfast to the poor family and are happy. They return home and eat bread and milk but are content.
- Later, the girls enact a play and it comes to an abrupt end, when the folding cot suddenly closes where their audiences have been sitting. No one is hurt but there is lots of laughter.
- Marmee surprises the girls with an elaborate supper. Seeing the delight on their faces, Marmee tells them that Old Mr Laurence has sent this feast for them when he learnt about the selfless thing the girls did for the Hummels in the morning.

# Chapter 3

'Jo! Where are you?' cried Meg, standing at the foot of the garret stairs.

'Here!' answered Jo who sat wrapped up in a comforter, by the sunny window, eating apples and crying over a sad description in the book.

'An invitation from Mrs Gardiner for tomorrow night!' cried Meg and then proceeded to read it with girlish delight. "Mrs Gardiner would be happy to see Miss Margaret and Miss Josephine at a little dance on New Year's Eve." Marmee has allowed us to go, now what shall we wear?'

'What's the use of asking, when you know we have only our poplins?' asked Jo. 'Our poplins are nice enough for us. Yours is as good as new! Mine has a burnt patch and a tear. What shall I do? It shows badly!'

'You must sit still and keep your back out of sight. The front is all right!'

Soon, the two young girls were ready for the party. They looked good in their simple suits. Meg's high-heeled slippers were hurtfully tight though she would not own it and Jo's nineteen hairpins seemed stuck straight into her head, which was not exactly comfortable!

'Have a good time, dears!' said Mrs March, as the sisters walked down the walk. 'I will send Hannah to fetch you at eleven.'

'Thanks Marmee, now Jo, remember to be poised!' said Meg.

'I know I shall forget all your instructions. If you see me doing anything wrong, just wink at me,' returned Jo.

'Winking isn't ladylike. I'll lift my eyebrows if anything is wrong and nod if you are all right.'

Mrs Gardiner, a stately old lady, greeted them kindly and handed them over to the eldest of her six daughters. Meg knew Sallie and was soon at ease but Jo didn't care much for girls or girlish gossip.

She stood with her back carefully against the wall and felt completely out of place. She could not roam about and amuse herself, for the burnt patch on her dress would show, so she stared at people when the dancing began.

Meg was asked for a dance at once and the tight slippers tripped about so briskly that none would have guessed the pain she felt. Jo saw a big red headed youth walking towards her corner. Fearing that he meant to ask her for a dance, she slipped into a curtained recess, intending to peep and enjoy herself in peace. Unfortunately, another bashful person had chosen the same refuge, for, as the curtain fell behind her, she found herself face to face with the 'Laurence boy'.

'Dear me, I didn't know someone was here!' stammered Jo.

The boy looked a little startled but he pleasantly laughed and said, 'You could stay here if you like.'

'Won't I disturb you?'

'Not a bit. I only came here because I don't know many people and felt rather strange.'

The boy sat down and Jo, trying to be polite, said, 'I think you live near us, don't you?'

'Next door,' and he laughed freely.

That put Jo at ease and she said, 'We had such a good time over your nice Christmas present.'

'Grandpa sent it.'

'Wasn't it your idea?'

'How is your cat, Miss March?' asked the boy, trying to look sober while his black eyes shone with fun.

'Good, thank you, Mr Laurence but I am not Miss March, I'm only Jo,' returned the young lady.

'I'm not Mr Laurence, I'm only Laurie. Don't you like to dance, Miss Jo?' asked Laurie.

'I like it well enough if there is plenty of space and everyone is lively. In a place like this, I'm sure to tread on people's toes, or do something dreadful, so I keep out of mischief and let Meg sail about.

Laurie and Jo chatted and felt like old acquaintances. Laurie's bashfulness soon wore off and because her dress was forgotten, Jo was her merry self again. She liked the 'Laurence boy' better than ever.

Just then she remarked, 'That's a splendid polka! Why don't you go and try it?'

'If you come,' he answered, with a gallant little bow.

'I can't because...' and Jo stopped, undecided whether to tell or to laugh.

'Because, what?'

'You won't tell anyone?'

'Never!'

'Well, my frock has a burnt patch and if I dance, it will show. Meg told me to keep still so no one would see it.'

Laurie paused for a minute before saying, 'Never mind. There's a big hall over there where we can dance gaily and no one will see us. Let's go!'

The hall was empty and they had a grand polka, for Laurie danced well and taught her the German step, which, being full of swing and spring, delighted Jo. When the music stopped, they sat down on the stairs to get their breath. Just then Meg appeared in search of her sister. She looked very pale and in pain.

'I've sprained my ankle. It aches so badly that I can hardly stand. I don't know how will I ever walk back home!' she said. 'Besides, it is past nine and very dark. I'll rest till Hannah comes and then do the best I can.' Laurie who was sitting there, offered to help them and brought a cup of coffee for Meg. He was so helpful that even Meg pronounced him a 'nice boy'. They had a merry time till Hannah appeared.

Hannah scolded, Meg cried when Jo decided to take things into her own hands.

At this moment, Laurie offered to take them home in his grandfather's carriage. They thanked Laurie and crept in quietly, hoping not to disturb anyone.

◆

When Mr March lost his property in trying to help an unfortunate friend, the two oldest girls begged to be allowed to do something toward their own support, at least. Margaret found a place as a nursery governess. Jo happened to suit Aunt March, who was lame and needed an active person to wait upon her. The childless old lady fancied Jo's blunt manners and had offered to take her for a companion. This did not really suit Jo but she accepted and, to everyone's surprise, got on remarkably well with her irascible relative. The real attraction, for Jo, was a large library of fine books, which was left to dust and spiders after Uncle March's death.

Meg was Amy's confidant and by some strange attraction of opposites, Jo was gentle Beth's. The two older girls were greatly attached to one another but both watched over the younger sisters in their own way. And each evening, they all sat together recalling all the stories of the day.

## Chapter Highlights

- Jo and Meg are invited to a dance by Mrs Gardiner, their neighbour, in the evening. The girls go to the dance, Jo with many pins stuck in her head and a burnt patch on the back of her dress and Meg in shoes a little tight for her.
- While Meg is soon dancing, Jo, worried about the burnt patch and from the fear that someone will ask her for dance, quickly retreats into an empty recess. To her surprise, she finds herself face to face with the 'Laurence Boy'.
- Jo and the boy called Laurie soon start talking. She learns that it was his grandfather's idea to send them the feast on Christmas Day. Jo says that they were grateful for it.
- After a while, Laurie asks her why she is away from the dance floor. Reluctantly, Jo tells him about the burnt patch on her dress. Laurie suggests that they can go into the empty hall there and dance and no one will see them. Jo agrees and they dance together.
- In some time, Meg comes along complaining that she has hurt her ankle and that she must rest now before Hannah comes to take them back home.
- When Hannah does come, Laurie offers that the girls can go home in his carriage. Meg is relieved and Jo is glad.
- We later learn that the two eldest girls, Meg and Jo support themselves. Meg works as a nursery governess while Jo attends to their Aunt March. She is an old, lame lady who is rich but childless and wants someone to look after her. Jo decided to become her companion only because the old lady has a large library.

# Chapter 4

'What are you going to do now, Jo?' asked Meg one snowy afternoon, as her sister came tramping through the hall, in rubber boots, with a broom in one hand and a shovel in the other.

'I can't keep still all day. I like adventure and I'm going to find some,' and Jo went back to clear the snow from the paths. The snow was light and with her broom she soon swept a path all round the garden. A garden separated the Marches' house from that of Mr Laurence. On one side was an old, brown house, looking rather bare and shabby, robbed of the vines that in summer covered its walls and the flowers. On the other side was a stately stone mansion, indicative of every sort of comfort and luxury, from the big coach house and well-kept grounds to the conservatory. Yet it seemed a lonely house, for no children frolicked on the lawn, no motherly face ever smiled at the windows, and few people went in and out, except the old gentleman and his grandson.

She longed to see the hidden glories inside the mansion and to know Laurie, and it seemed that he would like to be known too, but he did not know how to begin. Also, he had not been seen lately. Jo began to think he had gone away when one day, she saw a brown face at an upper window, looking wistfully down into their garden, where Beth and Amy were throwing snowballs at one another.

'That boy is suffering due to lack of friends and fun,' thought Jo to herself. 'He needs company of jolly kids to play with. I guess I should go and tell his grandpa.' The idea amused the daring Jo, who always scandalized Meg by her queer antics. The plan of 'going over' was not forgotten. When a snowy afternoon came, Jo resolved to try what could be done. She saw Mr Lawrence drive off. All was quiet, servants out of sight and nothing human was visible except a curly black head leaning on a thin hand, at the upper window.

'There he is,' thought Jo, 'I'll toss a snowball, make him look out and then say a kind word to him,' and she threw a small ball of soft snow, and the head turned at once, showing a face which lost its listless look in a minute, as the big eyes brightened and the mouth began to smile. Jo nodded and called out, 'Hello! Are you sick?'

Laurie opened the window, and croaked, 'Better, thank you. I've had a bad cold and been shut up for a week.'

'Ask someone to come and spend some time with you then.'

'There isn't anyone I'd like to see. Boys make such a row and my head is still weak.'

'Isn't there some nice girl who'd read and amuse you? Girls are quiet and like to play nurse.'

'Don't know any.'

'You know us,' replied Jo, laughingly.

'So I do! Will you come, please?' cried Laurie. 'I'm not quiet and nice but I'll come, if Mother allows me. Shut the window and wait till I come.'

Laurie was very excited at the thought of interesting company. Soon, Jo stood in the Laurence parlour with a covered dish in one hand and Beth's three kittens in the other.

'Here I am, bag and baggage,' she said briskly. 'Mother sent her love and was glad if I could do anything for you. Meg sent you some of her blancmange, she makes it very nicely, and Beth thought her cats would be comforting.'

It so happened that Beth's funny bone was just the thing, for in laughing over the kittens, Laurie forgot his bashfulness at once.

'Shall I read something to you?' said Jo looking at the tempting books kept nearby.

'Thank you! I've read all those! We would rather talk,' suggested Laurie.

'Great! I'll talk all day. Beth says I don't know when to stop.'

'Is Beth the rosy one, who stays at home and sometimes, goes out with a little basket?' asked Laurie with interest.

'Yes, that's Beth.'

'The pretty one is Meg, and the curly-haired one is Amy, I guess?'

'How did you find that out?'

Laurie blushed but answered frankly, 'I often hear you calling to one another and when I'm alone up here, I can't help looking over at your house, you always seem to be having so much fun. I am sorry but sometimes you forget to put down the curtain at the window and when the lamps are lighted, it's like looking at a picture with you all around the table with your mother. Her face is right opposite and it looks so sweet behind the flowers, I can't help looking at it. I haven't got any mother, you know,' said Laurie poking the fire to hide his sadness.

The sadness in his eyes touched Jo's heart. At fifteen, she was innocent and frank as a child and there was no nonsense in her head. Laurie was lonely, she realized. Her face was very friendly as she said, 'We'll never draw that curtain and you can look as much as you like. I just wish, you'd come over instead. Would your grandpa allow you?'

'I think he would, if your mother asked him. He's very kind and lets me do what I like, only he's afraid I might be a bother to strangers,' replied Laurie.

'We are neighbours and you can never be a bother.'

Just then, a bell rang. Jo stood up in alarm, 'Mercy me! It's your grandpa!'

'Well, what if it is? You aren't afraid of anyone,' added Laurie, looking wicked.

'I think I am a little bit afraid of him though I don't know why I should be. I have Mummy's permission and I don't think you're bad company,' said Jo, composing herself, though she kept looking at the entrance.

'The doctor to see you, sir,' said the maid.

'Excuse me! I'll be back in a few minutes,' said Laurie.

'Don't worry about me. I'm happy here,' answered Jo.

Laurie went away and Jo amused herself by standing before a fine portrait of the old gentleman when the door opened again and without turning, she said decidedly, 'I'm sure that I shouldn't be afraid of him. He's got kind eyes, though his mouth is grim and he seems to have tremendous willpower. He isn't as handsome as my grandfather but I like him.'

'Thank you, ma'am,' said a gruff voice behind her and she turned around in great dismay to see old Mr Laurence, standing there.

Jo blushed. A wild desire to run away possessed her but that would be cowardly. So she resolved to stay and face the consequences.

A second look showed her that the living eyes, under the bushy eyebrows, were kinder than the painted ones and there was a twinkle in them. In a gruff voice, the old gentleman said, 'So you're not afraid of me?'

'Not really, sir.'

'You don't find me as handsome as your grandfather?'

'Yes sir, that's true!'

'And I've got a tremendous will, have I?'

'I only said I thought so.'

'But you like me in spite of it?'

'Yes, I do, sir.'

That answer pleased the old gentleman. He laughed and shook hands with her. Then, he added, 'You've got your grandfather's spirit, though you haven't his face. He was a fine man; he was brave and honest! I was proud to be his friend.'

'Thank you, sir,' and Jo was quite comfortable after that.

'What have you been doing to this boy of mine?' was the next question.

'Only trying to be a good neighbour, sir,' and Jo told him why she had planned to visit Laurie.

'You think he needs cheering up?'

'Yes, sir, he seems a little lonely and would benefit from company. We are only girls but we should be glad to help if we could, for we remember the splendid Christmas present you sent us,' said Jo eagerly.

'Oh that was the boy's idea. Tell your mother I shall come and visit her some day. There's the tea bell! Let's go down and continue to be good neighbours.' As Mr Laurence and Jo went down for tea, they met Laurie, who accompanied them.

The old gentleman did not say much as he drank his tea but he watched the young people, who chatted away like old friends. The change in his grandson did not escape him.

'Jo's right, the lad is lonely. I'll see what these little girls can do for him,' thought Mr Laurence, as he looked and listened.

Later that evening when all the afternoon's adventures had been told, the family thought that they must visit the Laurences.

Later, mother told the girls that Laurie's father had married an Italian lady, and that both died had when Laurie was a baby and that was when his grandfather took him under his care.

## Chapter Highlights

- One day, feeling restless, Jo decides to clear the snow from the path leading to their house. While doing so, she sees the difference between their house and that of the Laurence's, which are separated by a hedge. She notices that while their house looks bare, their neighbour's speaks of the luxury within those walls.
- She remembers that she has not seen Laurie after that dance. She wishes to go inside and talk to Laurie.
- One day, she sees Laurie looking out through a window into their garden where Beth and Amy are throwing snowballs at each other.
- Jo realizes that Laurie looks lonely and that he needs companions. Later, when she sees Mr Laurence drive off, daring Jo decides to go and meet Laurie.
- Seeing no one around, she tosses a snowball at Laurie. Laurie, at once, brightens up. He says that due to a bad cold he had been shut up but would like some company. Jo replies that she will come if Marmee allows her. Laurie is happy.
- In no time, Jo is inside the mansion. She has Beth's three kittens with her and Meg sends blancmange for him. In no time, Laurie has forgotten his sickness and is laughing at the antics of the kittens.
- Soon Laurie confesses that when he is lonely he often looks towards their house where he finds them surrounding their mother and having so much fun. Jo sees his loneliness and suggests that instead of looking at them, he can come and join in the fun.

- Laurie says that he can come if his grandfather allows him to and that he will allow him if their mother asks him. He mentions that his grandfather is kind and lets him do what he wants but he does not want him to be a bother to anyone. Jo remarks that they are neighbours and that he can never be a bother to them.
- Just then, the doctor comes to see Laurie and he excuses himself. Jo, left to herself, looks at the portrait of the old gentleman. Just then, the door opens and without turning, she says that the old man has kind eyes, that he is not as handsome as her grandfather but she likes him and is not afraid of him.
- A gruff voice says thank you and Jo is startled. It is old Mr Laurence, Laurie's grandfather.
- The next moment, the old gentleman laughs out loud and tells her that her grandfather was brave, honest and that he is proud to be his friend. He later asks her what brought her to his house.
- Jo says that she was being a good neighbour and had come to see Laurie as he seemed lonely. She also mentions that it will do him good if he has company.
- Later, over tea, Mr Laurence observes that his grandson and Jo are talking like old friends and that the change has done him good.

# Chapter 5

When the March family visited Mr Laurence, they found the big house beautiful! They found that Mr Laurence was truly grateful for Mrs March's motherly affection, their cheerful company and the comfort Laurie felt in that humble home. So they soon forgot their pride and interchanged kindness without any barriers.

Everyone liked Laurie and he shared with his tutor that 'the Marches were regularly splendid girls.' With the delightful enthusiasm of youth, they took the solitary boy into their midst and he found something truly fascinating in the innocent companionship of these girls. Never having known mother or sisters, he was quick to feel the influences they brought about him. He was tired of books and found them so interesting that Mr Brooke often found Laurie playing truant and running over to the Marches.

What good times they had: Plays, sleigh rides, skating, pleasant evenings in the old parlour, frequent little parties at the great house, Meg's walks in the conservatory, Jo's browsing over the new library voraciously. Amy copied pictures and enjoyed beauty to her heart's content, and Laurie played 'lord of the manor' in the most delightful style.

Though Beth longed to play the grand piano, she could not gather courage to go ahead. She once went with Jo but the old gentleman, stared at her hard and said 'Hey!' so loud, that he frightened her greatly. No enticements could overcome her fear.

Finally, Mr Laurence set about mending matters. During one of the brief calls he made to the Marches, he artfully led the conversation to music. Beth found it impossible to stay in her distant corner, but inched nearer, completely fascinated.

Purposely ignoring her, Mr Laurence talked on about Laurie's lessons and teachers. He told Mrs March, 'The boy neglects his music now and the piano suffers for want of use. Wouldn't some of your girls like to practise on it, just to keep it in tune, Ma'am?'

Beth took a step forward as the thought of practising on that splendid instrument nearly took her breath away. Without waiting for a reply, Mr Laurence spoke on with a smile, 'They needn't speak to anyone but run in at any time for I'm shut up in my study at the other end of the house, Laurie is out a great deal.'

As he rose to leave, he added, 'Please, convey this to the young ladies and if they don't care to come, never mind.' Just then a little hand slipped into his and Beth looked up at him with a face full of gratitude, as she said, in her earnest yet timid way, 'Oh sir, they do care, very much!'

'So you are the one who is fond of music?' he asked, as he looked down at her very kindly.

'I'm Beth. I love it dearly and I'll come, if you are quite sure nobody would be disturbed,' she added.

'The house is empty half the day, so come and play the piano as much as you like. I shall be obliged to you.'

Beth was no longer frightened. The old gentleman softly stroked the hair off her forehead and stooping down, he kissed her, saying, 'I had a little girl once, with eyes like these. God bless you, my dear! Good day, madam,' and he left in a great hurry.

Beth was rapturous. Next day, Beth made her way to the grand piano. Quite by accident, of course, some pretty, easy music lay on the piano and with trembling fingers Beth touched the great instrument. In no time she forgot her fear, herself and everything else but the unspeakable delight which music gave her.

After that, the great drawing room was haunted by a tuneful spirit that came and went unseen. She never knew that Mr Laurence opened his study door to hear the old-fashioned airs he liked and that the servants were asked to keep away.

'Mother, I'm going to make a pair of slippers for Mr Laurence. He is so kind to me, I must thank him and I don't know any other way. Can I do it?' asked Beth, a few weeks later. Mother readily agreed for Beth seldom asked for anything.

Soon, the slippers were ready.

Then Beth wrote a short note and with Laurie's help, got them smuggled onto the study table one morning before the old gentleman was up.

When this excitement was over, Beth waited to see what would happen. On the afternoon of the second day, as she came home several joyful voices could be heard screaming, 'A letter from the old gentleman! Come quick and read it!'

Beth hurried and was received by her sisters' saying in unison, 'Look there!' Beth saw and turned pale with delight, for there stood a little cabinet piano, with a letter lying on its glossy lid, addressed to 'Miss Elizabeth March.'

'You read it! I can't, I feel so queer! Oh, it is too lovely!' said Beth, quite overwhelmed.

Jo opened the note and began to laugh, when she read the first words:

Miss March:

'Dear Madam,
I have had many pairs of slippers in my life but I never had any that suited me so well. Heart's-ease is my favourite flower and these will always remind me of the gentle giver.

I like to pay my debts, so I know you will allow 'the old gentleman' to send you something which once belonged to the little granddaughter he lost.

With hearty thanks and best wishes, I remain

Your grateful friend and humble servant,

JAMES LAURENCE.'

'Beth, that's an honour to be proud of! Laurie told me how fond Mr Laurence used to be of the child who died and how he kept all her little things carefully. Just think, he's given you her piano!' said Jo.

Beth lovingly touched the beautiful black and white keys and pressed the bright pedals.

'You should go and thank Mr Laurence,' said Jo.

Quickly, Beth walked through the hedge to the Laurences' house. She knocked and entered the study. Then, without saying anything she embraced the old gentleman. The old gentleman was astonished but he liked it immensely. He was so touched and pleased by an affectionate kiss that all his gruffness vanished. He felt as if he had got his own little granddaughter back again. Beth ceased to fear him from that moment.

## Chapter Highlights

- The March family pays a visit to the mansion and the old Mr Laurence is truly grateful to Mrs March for her affection and to the girls. Laurie who had never known family, loved them and was fascinated by them. His tutor, Mr Brooke, now often finds Laurie at the Marches' house.
- Laurie and girls have a good time. They play together and

the girls often pay visit to the manor. Beth longs to play the grand piano but she is scared of Mr Laurence.

- One day, the old gentleman pays a visit to the Marches. There, he gradually turns the conversation to music. Beth is interested at once. The old gentleman pays her no heed on purpose as he talks about Laurie's lessons and his teachers.
- He says that Laurie neglects his music and therefore if any of the girls want to practice on it, just to keep it in tune, they are welcome to do so.
- Unable to wait anymore, Beth slips her hand into the old gentleman's hand and says that she will be delighted to come.
- The next day, Beth goes to the manor and with trembling hands starts playing thc piano. As she is enraptured by the music, she doesn't realize that old Mr Laurence is listening to the music she is playing and likes it.
- To thank Mr Laurence, she makes slippers for him and smuggles them into his study with the help of Laurie.
- One afternoon, when Beth comes home, she hears delighted voices all around. There is a letter from the old gentleman. And when she enters the house, she gasps. There is a cabinet piano sitting in the room and it is for her.
- Another moment and Beth is hurrying along the hedge towards the manor to thank Mr Laurence. She rushes to the study and without saying a word, embraces the old man. Surprised but happy, Mr Laurence feels fells as if he has found his granddaughter back. Beth no longer fears the old gentleman.

## Chapter 6

'Hey, where are you two off to?' asked Amy.

'Don't bother!' replied Jo sharply.

Insulted, Amy turned to Meg, who never refused her anything and coaxed, 'Please tell me! I should like to go with you. I am so lonely.'

Jo added impatiently, 'You can't go, Amy, so stop whining.'

'I know you are going with Laurie.'

'Yes, we are. Now stop bothering.'

Amy saw Meg slip a fan into her pocket and she howled, 'I know, you're going to the theatre to see the "Seven Castles!" I shall go. It was unfair of you two not to tell me earlier.'

'Be a good child,' said Meg soothingly.

'Laurie won't like it and it will be very rude to drag in Amy, for he invited only us!' Amy began to cry. Just then, Laurie called from below and the two girls left, leaving behind a wailing Amy. Amy shouted from behind, 'You'll be sorry for this, Jo!'

They had a charming time, for 'The Seven Castles of the Diamond Lake' was a wonderful play.

When they got home, they found Amy reading in the parlour. She never lifted her eyes from her book or asked a single question. Jo looked around and found all her things in order, so she decided that Amy had forgotten all about it but she was mistaken, for the very next day she discovered something which produced a tempest.

Meg, Beth and Amy were sitting together, late in the afternoon, when Jo burst into the room, breathlessly demanding, 'Has anyone taken my book?'

Meg and Beth said 'No' at once but Amy said nothing. Jo saw her colour rise and so she turned to her, 'Amy, you know where it is! You better tell me!'

'I have burnt it!' screamed Amy.

'What! You burnt my little book which was my life! I meant to finish before Father returned home?' asked Jo, turning very pale.

'Yes, I did! I told you I'd make you pay for being so rude and I have!'

Jo's hot temper possessed her. She shook Amy till she cried out in pain and fear.

When Mrs March learnt about it, she was grieved. Amy felt that no one would love her till she sought her sister's pardon. She regretted her act. No one spoke, not even Mrs March, for they all knew that when Jo was in that mood, words were of no use!

As Jo marched off to bed, she muttered, 'Since everybody is so hateful, I'll ask Laurie to join me for skating. He is always kind and jolly.' Next morning, off Jo went.

Amy heard the clash of skates and looked out with an impatient remark, 'There she goes without me! She had promised to take me with her next time, for this is the last ice we shall have this season but she is so angry with me!'

'Don't blame her for that. You were in the wrong,' said Meg. 'Go after them. Don't say anything till Jo has regained her good humour in Laurie's company.

I'm sure she'll forgive you!'

Amy nodded. She got ready in great excitement and ran after Jo and Laurie.

It was not far to the river but both were already there when Amy reached. Jo saw her coming but completely ignored her.

Laurie did not see her. He was carefully skating along the bank, checking out the ice, for there had been a warm spell.

As Laurie turned the bend, he shouted back, 'Keep near the bank. It isn't safe in the middle.' Jo heard him but Amy missed the warning. Jo glanced over her shoulder and said to herself, 'I don't care whether Amy heard or not, let her take care of herself.'

Laurie had vanished round the bend, Jo was at the curve and Amy was far behind, striking out toward the smoother ice in the middle of the river. For a minute Jo stood still. Something made her turn round, just in time to see Amy throw up her hands and go down, with a sudden crash of thin ice, the splash of water, and a cry that made Jo's heart freeze. Jo stood motionless with a terror-stricken face, staring at the little blue hood above the water.

All of a sudden, something rushed past her and she heard Laurie's voice call out, 'Bring a rail, quick!'

For the next few minutes, Jo worked as if possessed, blindly obeying Laurie, who was lying flat, held Amy up by his arm and hockey stick and together they got the child out, more frightened than hurt.

They got the shivering, dripping and crying Amy home as fast as they could. She was wrapped in blankets before a hot fire, where she fell asleep. During all this, Jo had scarcely spoken but she looked pale and disturbed. Then, as penitent tears rolled down Jo's cheeks, she told her mother everything. Marmee held Jo all the while. Amy stirred and sighed in her sleep.

'How could I be so wicked?' said Jo, softly stroking her sister's wet hair.

Just then, Amy opened her eyes. Neither said a word but they hugged one another and everything was forgiven and forgotten.

## Chapter Highlights

- A few days later, Amy finds Meg and Jo all dressed up and ready to go out. Feeling lonely, Amy wants to accompany them but as Laurie has invited the two girls to watch a play they could not take her along. But the young Amy could not take being left behind. She is particularly upset with Jo.
- Later, when the girls return, they find Amy reading and she never asks them anything about the play. Jo thinks that Amy has forgotten the incident but she is mistaken.
- Next morning, Jo finds her book missing. Soon, she learns that Amy has burnt it. Jo is angry with Amy. When Mrs March learns of the incident, she is grieved. Amy is repentant but is afraid to seek Jo's pardon.
- The next day, she sees Jo and Laurie going out to skate over the frozen river. She follows them behind on her skates. Jo notices her but ignores her and Laurie does not see her.
- Laurie goes carefully over the frozen river and says that they should avoid going near the middle. Jo hears it but Amy doesn't. Following Jo at a distance, Amy goes towards the middle of the water body. Suddenly, Jo hears a voice. She looks over her shoulder and freezes.
- Amy had trodden on thin ice and fallen into the icy depths. Jo can only see her hands out of the water and is terror-stricken. However, Laurie's timely action saves Amy.
- Together, Jo and Laurie bring the dripping and frightened Amy home. She lies covered in blankets before the fireplace. Jo is filled with remorse for being evil. She confesses everything to Marmee.
- Just then, Amy opens her eyes and without exchanging a single word, Jo and Amy embrace each other. Everything is forgiven between them.

## Chapter 7

Jo had confined herself in the garret. For nearly three hours, she sat, writing busily, her papers spread all over. Jo scribbled away till the last page was filled, when she signed her name with a flourish and threw down her pen, exclaiming,

'There, I've done my best! If this won't suit I shall have to wait till I can do better.'

Lying on the sofa, she carefully read through the manuscript, making a few changes here and there. Then she tied it up with a smart red ribbon and sat a minute looking at it with a sober, wistful expression, which plainly showed how earnest her work had been. In her desk, Jo kept her papers and a few books, safely shut away. From here, Jo produced another manuscript and putting both in her pocket, crept quietly downstairs.

She put on her hat and jacket as noiselessly as possible, slipped out of her house and soon found herself on the road. Once there, she hailed a passing omnibus and rolled away to town.

On alighting from the bus, she went off at a great pace till she reached a certain number in a certain busy street. Having found the place with some difficulty, she went into the doorway, looked up the dirty stairs, and after standing stock still for a minute, suddenly dived into the street and walked away as rapidly as she came. A young gentleman, watching this peculiar behaviour, at some distance, put on his coat, took his hat and went down to post himself in the opposite doorway, saying with a smile, 'It's like her to come alone, but if she has a bad time she'll need someone to help her home.'

Ten minutes later, Jo came running downstairs with a very red face and the general appearance of a person who had just passed through a trying ordeal of some sort. When she saw the young gentleman she looked very pleased.

He asked with a touch of sympathy, 'Did you have a bad time?'

'Not really!'

'You got through quickly.'

'Yes, thank goodness!'

'Why did you go alone?'

'Didn't want anyone to know.'

'I'd like to hear the interesting news immensely.'

'Well! It's a secret and must be kept that way!'

'I promise! Now, tell me!'

'Well, I've left two stories with a newspaperman for publishing. He would tell me next week if he would publish them,' whispered Jo.

'Hurrah for Miss March, the celebrated American author!' cried Laurie.

'Hush! I couldn't rest without trying but I haven't told anyone yet because I don't want anyone else to be disappointed.'

'It won't fail, Jo, your stories are works of Shakespeare compared to the rubbish that is published every day. Won't it be fun to see them in print? Shan't we feel proud of you?'

Jo's eyes sparkled, for it is always pleasant to be believed in and a friend's praise is truly sweet! 'Let's race down this hill!' suggested Laurie.

After a while, breathless and with dishevelled hair Jo was sitting by a tree trunk. Laurie was collecting Jo's straw hat when Meg passed by.

'What in the world are you doing here?' she asked, regarding her dishevelled sister with surprise.

'Collecting leaves,' Jo replied meekly, sorting the rosy handful she had just swept up.

'And brown straw hats,' added Laurie. 'They grow on this road, Meg.'

'You have been running, Jo. How could you? When will you stop such romping ways?' said Meg reprovingly.

'Never till I'm stiff and old and have to use a crutch. Don't try to make me grow up before my time, Meg. Let me be a little girl as long as I can.'

For a week or so, Jo behaved strangely which confused the sisters. She rushed to the door when the postman rang. Laurie and she were always making signs to one another and talking about 'Spread Eagles' till the girls declared they had both lost their wits. One day, as Meg sat sewing at her window, she was scandalized to see Laurie chasing Jo all over the garden and finally capturing her. Meg could not see much but shrieks of laughter were heard, followed by the murmur of voices and a great flapping of newspapers.

In a few minutes Jo bounced in, lay down on the sofa and began to read.

'Have you anything interesting there?' asked Meg.

'Nothing but a story, I guess,' returned Jo, carefully keeping the name of the paper out of sight.

'Read it,' said Meg.

After a long deep breath, Jo began to read the story. The girls listened with interest.

'Viola and Angelo are two of our favourite names, isn't that queer?' said Meg.

'Who wrote it?' asked Beth, who had caught a different look on Jo's face.

Jo suddenly sat up, put the paper aside, and displaying a flushed countenance, replied, 'Your sister!'

'You?' cried Meg, dropping her work.

'Oh Jo, I am so proud!' exclaimed Beth and ran to hug her sister.

How delighted they all were! Beth and Amy skipped and danced with joy. Hannah too joined in the celebration. Mrs March was really proud of her daughter! Jo was elated as the paper was passed from hand to hand.

'Tell us about it.' 'When did it come?' 'How much did you get for it?' cried the family, all in one breath as they clustered about Jo, for these foolish, affectionate people made a jubilee of every little household joy.

'Stop jabbering, girls, and I'll tell you everything,' said Jo. Jo was overwhelmed and shed some happy tears, for to be independent and earn the praise of those she loved were the dearest wishes of her heart, and this seemed to be the first step toward that happy end.

## Chapter Highlights

- Jo has been writing for three hours straight in the garret. When she is done, she carefully reads it, makes changes in it and then ties it up with a ribbon. After a while, she puts it inside her pocket, goes out of the house and takes a bus to town.
- Once there, she goes to a certain street and enters a certain building. As she enters the building, she is seen by a man who, amused by her reactions, follows her unseen and stands opposite to the building which Jo enters.

- Ten minutes later, when Jo comes out of the building, she sees the young man and is pleased. The young man is Laurie.
- Jo tells him that she has a secret and Laurie says that he will keep it that way until she wants to make it known.
- Jo, however, tells him that she has submitted two stories to a publisher for printing. She must wait a week before he gives her an answer. Laurie assures her that her stories will be published and then they race down the road.
- After a while, Meg finds both Laurie and Jo sitting by a tree trunk. Meg asks Jo to act ladylike. Jo replies to let her remain so.
- Over the next week, Jo keeps rushing to the postman to know if any post has come for her. The sisters are confused by Jo's behaviour.
- Suddenly, one day as Meg is busy with her sewing and others are sitting by, Jo rushes in with a newspaper. Jo asks her to read the story in the paper, but instead Meg asks her to read it out to them.
- Jo's sisters appreciate the story and ask who has written it. Jo reveals that she has written it. The sisters are filled with happiness while Mrs March is really proud of her. Jo then tells them how it had all come about.

## Chapter 8

'November is the most disagreeable month in the whole year,' said Margaret, looking out at the frostbitten garden.

Jo groaned and leaned both elbows on the table in a despondent attitude. Beth, who sat at the other window said, smiling, 'Two pleasant things are going to happen right away. Marmee is coming down the street and Laurie is tramping through the garden as if he had an exciting plan!'

In they both came, and Laurie said, 'Won't some of you come for a drive? I've been working away at mathematics and am exhausted. Come on girls!'

'Much obliged, but I'm busy.' And Meg whisked out her workbasket, for she was following her mother's advice that it was best, for her at least, not to drive too often with the young gentleman.

'Can I do anything for you, Madam Mother?' asked Laurie, leaning over Mrs March's chair with the affectionate look and tone he always gave her.

'No, thank you, except call at the post office. It's our day for a letter and the postman hasn't appeared so far.'

A sharp ring interrupted her and a minute later, Hannah came.

'It's one of those horrid telegraphs,' she said, handling it as if she was afraid it would explode.

At the word 'telegraph', Mrs March snatched it, read the two lines it contained, and dropped into her chair as white as the little paper she held.

Laurie dashed downstairs for water, while Meg and Hannah supported her and Jo read aloud, in a frightened voice,

Mrs March:
Your husband is very ill. Come at once.
S. HALE
Blank Hospital, Washington.

The room suddenly became very still as they listened breathlessly, the day darkened and suddenly the whole world seemed to change, as the girls gathered about their mother, feeling as if all the happiness and support of their lives was about to be withdrawn.

Mrs March soon recovered, read the message again and stretched out her arms to her daughters, saying, in a tone they never forgot, 'I shall go at once but it may be too late. Dear children, help me to bear it!'

Quickly, Hannah and Meg packed a trunk for their mother while Mrs March called Laurie.

'Send a telegram saying I will come at once. The next train goes early in the morning. I'll take that,' Mrs March instructed Laurie.

'What else? The horses are ready. I can go anywhere, do anything,' he said, eager to be of use.

'Leave a note at Aunt March's. Jo, give me that pen and paper.'

Mrs March needed to borrow money for the journey from Aunt March.

'Jo, tell Mrs King that I can't come. On the way get these things. They'll be needed and I must go prepared for nursing. Beth, ask Mr Laurence for a couple of bottles of old wine.'

Mr Laurence came hurrying back with Beth, promising all

help in the protection of the girls during the mother's absence, which comforted her very much. There was nothing he didn't offer, from his own dressing gown to himself as escort.

However, Mrs March would not hear of the old gentleman undertaking the long journey! He saw the look, rubbed his hands and marched abruptly away, saying he'd be back in a while. No one had time to think of him again till Meg ran through the entry and almost collided with Mr Brooke.

'I'm very sorry to hear the news, Miss March,' he said, in the kind tone. 'I came to offer myself as escort to your mother. Mr Laurence has commissions in Washington and it will give me real satisfaction to be of service to her.'

Meg put out her hand, with a face so full of gratitude that Mr Brooke would have felt repaid for a much greater sacrifice.

'How kind you all are! Mother will accept, I'm sure and it will be such a relief to know that you are there to take care of her. Thank you, very much!'

Everything was arranged by the time Laurie returned with a note from Aunt March, enclosing the desired sum. The short afternoon wore away. All other errands were done. They began to get anxious as Jo was missing. She walked in with a very queer expression which puzzled the family as much as did the roll of bills she laid before her mother, saying in a choked voice, 'That's my contribution towards Father's recovery.'

'My dear, where did you get it? Twenty-five dollars! Jo,' asked the concerned mother.

'I didn't beg, borrow, or steal but I earned it and I don't think you'll blame me, for I only sold what was my own,' and she took off her bonnet. All were aghast for her abundant hair was cut short.

'Your beautiful hair! Oh, Jo, how could you? Dear, there was no need of this!' cried mother.

After supper all went to bed praying for the invalid.

In the cold grey dawn the sisters lit their lamp and read their chapter with an earnestness never felt before. For now the shadow of a real trouble had come, the little books were full of help and comfort and as they dressed, they agreed to say goodbye cheerfully and hopefully, and send their mother on her anxious journey without any tears.

The big trunk stood ready in the hall, Mother's cloak and bonnet lay on the sofa and Mother looked so pale with anxiety that the girls found it difficult to keep their resolution. Nobody talked as they waited for the carriage. Mrs March told the girls that they were being left to Hannah's care and Mr Laurence's protection. 'Don't grieve and fret when I am gone. Go on with your work as usual, for work is a blessed solace.'

'Yes, Mother.'

'Meg, dear, be prudent, watch over your sisters, consult Hannah, and take Mr Laurence's advice. Be patient, Jo, don't get despondent or do rash things, write to me and be my brave girl. Beth, comfort yourself with your music and be faithful to the little home duties. Amy, help all you can and be obedient.'

'We will, Mother!'

The rattle of an approaching carriage made them all start and listen. That was the hardest moment but the girls behaved. No one cried though their hearts were very heavy as they sent loving messages to Father. They kissed their mother quietly, and tried to wave their hands cheerfully when she drove away.

As she rolled away, the last thing she beheld as she turned the corner were the four bright faces, and behind them like a bodyguard, old Mr Laurence, faithful Hannah and devoted Laurie.

'How kind everyone is to us!' said Mrs March.

Later, when they went out to their daily tasks, the girls looked sorrowfully back at the window where they were accustomed to seeing their mother's face. Beth had remembered the little household ceremony and there she was, waving to them cheerfully.

'That's so like my Beth!' said Jo, waving her hat, with a grateful face.

Soon, news from their father comforted the girls very much, for though dangerously ill, the best and tenderest of nursing had begun to do him good.

Mr Brooke sent a bulletin every day. As the head of the family, Meg insisted on reading the dispatches, which grew cheerful as weeks passed.

## Chapter Highlights

- One dull day in November, Beth announces that two pleasant things are going to happen in the next few minutes. She has seen Marmee coming and Laurie dashing down their garden path.
- Laurie comes in and asks the girls if they would like to go for a ride in the motorcar. Just then Mrs March comes in. Meg refuses to go. In comes Hannah with a telegram.
- Seeing it, Mrs March snatches it from Hannah, reads it and drops down into a chair, white as a sheet. Laurie gets her water; Meg and Beth support her while Jo reads the telegram. It reads that Mr March is very ill and that Mrs March must come at once.
- The room is quite and it seems to the girls that the day has darkened and all their happiness has been sucked out. All preparations for the journey are quickly made.
- Hannah and Meg pack their mother's suitcase, Laurie goes with a telegram saying that she is coming at once

and another letter for Aunt March, from whom Mrs March borrows some money and Hannah is sent to Mr Laurence to ask him for some wine bottles.

- Mr Laurence comes rushing back. He says that he is sorry to hear of the sad news, that he will look after the girls, and that if Mrs March wishes, he can accompany her to Washington. Mrs March will not have the old gentleman travel so far. However, Mr Brooke soon comes along and says that he will accompany her and would like to be of service to her.
- Everyone is grateful for the kindness being done to them. Soon, Laurie comes with the desired money from Aunt March. Jo, however, is missing. When she does come, she walks up to Marmee and offers her money saying that this is her contribution to her expenses.
- Jo has cut her hair short to get the money.
- Early next day, the girls say goodbye to their mother. As the carriage rolls away, Marmee looks back and sees the girls surrounded by Mr Laurence, Hannah and devoted Laurie. She is pleased that the girls are in good hands.
- Soon, the girls receive a letter saying that their father is very ill but will soon be on the road to recovery. Over the next few days, gradually the news about their father brings good tidings for the girls' anxious hearts.

## Chapter 9

Everyone followed mother's advice, for a week but soon the girls relaxed as they were relieved of their first anxiety about their father.

It was only Beth who kept on, with only slight relapses into idleness or grieving.

Meanwhile, Beth went to nurse the baby of that desolate family to whom they had given away their Christmas breakfast. When she returned, she crept upstairs and shut herself into her mother's room.

Half an hour later, Jo went to 'Mother's closet' for something and found Beth sitting on the medicine chest, looking serious, with red eyes and a camphor bottle in her hand. Beth told Jo that the baby had died with scarlet fever. She was sent back home before she too could get the infection. But Beth is unwell. Hannah was told everything and she was in total control of the situation. She assured the two girls that there was no need to worry.

'We will have Dr Bangs take a look at you. Then we'll send Amy off to Aunt March's for some time, to keep her out of harm's way. One of you girls can stay at home and amuse Beth for a day or two. Which will you have, Beth?' asked Hannah.

'Jo, please,' said Beth.

'I'll go and tell Amy,' said Meg.

Amy rebelled outright. Meg reasoned, pleaded and

commanded but all in vain. Just when she went to ask Hannah, Laurie walked in to find Amy sobbing. She told her story, expecting to be consoled.

Laurie sat down beside Amy and said, 'Be a sensible little woman and do as they say. Don't cry, but hear what a jolly plan I've got. You go to Aunt March's and I'll come and take you out every day, driving or walking and we'll have a great time!'

This consoled Amy and she agreed to go to Aunt March's house. Everyone was delighted.

'How is the little dear?' asked Laurie, for Beth was his pet and he was really anxious about her.

'She is lying on Mother's bed! The baby's death has troubled her but I am hoping that she has only got cold. Hannah says she thinks so but she looks worried and that makes me nervous,' answered Meg.

'Tell me if you want me to telegraph to your mother?' asked Laurie.

'I think we ought to but Hannah says we mustn't. She says Mother can't leave Father and it will only cause tension. Beth won't be sick long!' said Meg.

'Hmm, what if you ask Grandfather after the doctor has examined Beth?' suggested Laurie.

'We will. Jo, go and get Dr Bangs at once,' commanded Meg. 'We can't decide anything till then!'

'Stay where you are, Jo. I'm the errand boy to this establishment,' said Laurie, taking up his cap.

Dr Bangs examined Beth and said that she had symptoms of the fever but he hoped that it would not be severe. Amy was ordered off at once, with Jo and Laurie as escort.

Beth was much sicker than what everyone suspected. The girls knew nothing about illness, so Hannah took control.

Jo devoted herself to Beth day and night. There came a time

when she was delirious and called imploringly for her mother. Jo grew frightened, Meg wanted to write to her mother when a letter from Washington added to their trouble, for Mr March had had a relapse and could not come home for a long while.

How dark the days seemed now, how sad and lonely the house, and how heavy were the hearts of the sisters as they worked and waited, while the shadow of death hovered over the once happy home.

Amy longed to be at home. Laurie haunted the house like a restless ghost and Mr Laurence locked the grand piano, because he could not bear to be reminded of the young neighbour who used to make the twilight pleasant for him. Everyone missed Beth.

The first of December was a wintry day; bitingly cold winds blew, snow fell. Dr Bangs looked long at Beth, saying, in a low voice to Hannah, 'If Mrs March can leave her husband she'd better be sent for.'

Hannah's lips twitched nervously, Meg dropped down into a chair as she lost her strength. Jo ran to the parlour, holding back her tears. Just then, Laurie came in with a letter, saying that Mr March was improving again. Jo read it thankfully but her face was so full of misery that Laurie asked, 'What is it? Is Beth worse?'

'I've sent for Mother; the doctor told us to,' said Jo.

'Oh, Jo, Beth is not as bad as that?' cried Laurie, startled.

'Yes, it is. She doesn't recognise us and doesn't talk like herself.'

'Poor girl, you're worn out. I telegraphed to your mother yesterday and Brooke answered she'd come at once. She'll be here tonight and everything will be fine! Aren't you glad?'

Laurie spoke very fast, turned red and excited, for he had kept his plot a secret. Jo flew out of her chair, stunned him by throwing her arms round his neck, with a joyful cry, 'Oh, Laurie! I am so glad!'

Laurie patted her back soothingly and finding that she was

recovering, followed it up by a bashful kiss or two, which brought Jo round at once. She put him gently away, saying, 'Oh, don't! I didn't mean to, it was dreadful of me, but you were such a dear that I couldn't help clinging to. Laurie, you're an angel! How shall I ever thank you?'

A breath of fresh air seemed to blow through the house and something better than sunshine brightened the quiet rooms. All day Jo and Meg hovered over Beth, watching, hoping and trusting in God and Mother. Finally, night came and the sisters sat looking at each other with brightening eyes, for help was near at hand. The doctor had been in to say that some change, for better or worse, would probably take place about midnight, at which time he would return.

The girls never forgot that night, for no sleep came to them as they kept their watch, with a numbing sense of helplessness.

It was past two, Jo was standing near the window when she heard a movement by the bed, and turning quickly, saw Meg kneeling before their mother's easy chair with her face hidden.

A dreadful fear seized Jo, as she thought, 'Beth is dead and Meg is afraid to tell me.'

Just then Hannah started out of her sleep, hurriedly looked at Beth, felt her hands, listened at her lips, and then, exclaimed in a whisper, 'She's sleeping naturally, her skin's damp and she breathes easy. Lord be praised!'

Just then the doctor came in and confirmed the good news.

Meg and Jo crept into the dark hall and held each other close, with hearts too full for words. Never had the sun risen so beautifully as it seemed to the heavy eyes of Meg and Jo, as they looked out in the early morning.

'Hark!' cried Jo, starting to her feet. Yes, there was a sound of bells at the door below, a cry from Hannah, and then Laurie's voice saying in a joyful whisper, 'Girls, she's come!'

## Chapter Highlights

- The girls behave well in their mother's absence. One day, Beth goes to nurse the baby of the Hummels whom the girls had given their breakfast. Meanwhile, Jo goes to 'Mother's Closet' to get something when she sees Beth sitting there with red eyes and a camphor bottle in her hand.
- Beth tells Jo that the baby has died from scarlet fever and that she was asked to return home lest she also catches it. Hannah is told everything and sends for Dr Bangs to take a look at Beth. She also decides to send Amy to Aunt March in order to keep her out of harm's way.
- Amy rebels. However, Laurie is able to persuade her to go to Aunt March.
- Laurie makes inquiries about Beth. Meg tells him that Beth is troubled because of the baby's death and Hannah says that she only has cold but the look in her eyes has worried her.
- Concerned and undecided if the girls should write to their mother, Laurie goes to fetch Dr Bangs. After his examination, the doctor says that Beth has symptoms of scarlet fever. Meg starts nursing Beth while Amy is at once sent to Aunt March's house escorted by Laurie and Jo.
- Hannah takes control of the situation. Jo attends to Beth's every need. Beth is much worse and there comes a time when the girls think of writing to their mother. But it is about that time that they receive a letter that their father has had a relapse and that Marmee will not be able to come for some time.
- The once happy house is still and filled with sadness. Laurie is restless and Mr Laurence shuts the grand piano as it

reminds him of the neighbour who had made his evenings pleasant. Everyone misses cheerful Beth.

- On the first day of December, Dr Bangs, after examining Beth, says that Mrs March should be sent for. Hannah and the girls are on the brink of tears.
- Just then Laurie comes in with news that Mr March has recovered significantly. Hearing about Beth startles Laurie. Jo also informs him that she has sent for their mother. Laurie then tells her that he had already sent for Mrs March and that she will reach soon.
- A breath of fresh air seems to pass through the house. The doctor too says that he will pay a visit at night to see if there is a change for the better.
- Around midnight, Jo and Amy see that Beth seems to be sleeping peacefully. Just then, the doctor also comes, examines Beth and confirms that the worst has passed and that Beth is on the road to recovery. The sisters are filled with happiness.
- As the first rays of sunshine spread across the horizon, Hannah hears bells and Laurie comes inside and says that Marmee has arrived.

## Chapter 10

The house was full of genuine happiness, for when Beth woke, her eyes fell on mother's face. Too weak to wonder at anything, she only smiled and nestled close in the loving arms about her. Then she slept again and the girls waited upon their mother.

Hannah had 'dished up' an amazing breakfast for mother, as her way of expressing excitement. Meg and Jo fed their mother, while they listened to her whispered account of Father's state and Mr Brooke's promise to stay and nurse him.

What a strange yet pleasant day that was. Feeling a blissful sense of burdens lifted off, Meg and Jo closed their weary eyes and lay at rest, like storm-beaten boats safe at anchor in a quiet harbour.

Mrs March would not leave Beth's side but rested in the big chair, waking often to look at and touch her child. That evening while Meg was writing to her father to report mother's safe arrival, Jo slipped into Beth's room and finding her mother in her usual place, stood before her with a worried gesture and an undecided look.

'What is it, dear?' asked Mrs March.

'I want to tell you something, Mother.'

'About Meg?'

'How quickly you guessed! Yes, it's about her, and though it's a small thing, it troubles me.'

'Speak softly and tell me!' replied Mrs March.

'Last summer Meg left a pair of gloves over at the Laurences' and only one was returned. We forgot about it, till Teddy told me that Mr Brooke has it and that he likes Meg but daren't say so, as she is so young and he so poor. Isn't that dreadful?'

'Do you think Meg cares for him?' asked Mrs March.

'I don't know anything about love and such nonsense!' cried Jo.

'Then you fancy that Meg is not interested in John?'

'Who?' cried Jo.

'Mr Brooke. I call him 'John' now. We fell into the way of doing so at the hospital and he likes it.'

'Oh, dear! He's been good to Father and you won't send him away but let Meg marry him, if she wants to,' added Jo in disgust.

'My dear, don't get angry with him. I will tell you how it happened. John went with me at Mr Laurence's request and was so devoted to dear Father that both of us couldn't help getting fond of him. He was perfectly open and honourable about Meg and told us that he loved her but would earn a comfortable home before he asked her to marry him. He only wanted our leave to love her. He is truly an excellent young man. We could not refuse to listen to him but also did not consent to Meg's engagement when she is so young.'

'I knew there was mischief brewing. I felt it and now it's worse than I imagined.'

This odd suggestion made Mrs March smile but she said gravely, 'Jo, I have confided in you but don't say anything to Meg yet. When John comes back, I see them together, I can judge better of her feelings toward him.'

'She's got such a soft heart; it will melt like butter in the sun if anyone looks sentimentally at her. She'll fall in love with him and that's the end of our peace, fun, and cozy times together. Oh, dear me!'

'Jo, it is natural and right. You should all go to homes of your own, in time but I do want to keep my girls as long as I can. I am sorry that this happened so soon, for Meg is only seventeen and it will take John some time before he can make a home for her. Your father and I have agreed that she shall not bind herself in any way, nor be married, before twenty.'

## Chapter Highlights

- The house is filled with happiness once more. Beth smiles seeing her mother. Jo and Meg can finally rest and Hannah, in order to show her excitement, prepares a splendid breakfast. The girls also learn that Mr Brooke is staying with their father and has assured Marmee that he will look after Mr March.
- Marmee stays by Beth's side and she is a comfort to her. Towards evening, while Meg is writing to their father about their mother's safe arrival, Jo approaches her mother with an uncertain look.
- When asked, she tells her mother that Meg and Mr Brooke are in love. She is concerned because Meg is so young and Mr Brooke is poor. Her mother tells her that she has herself grown fond of John Brooke.
- Her mother says that John has confessed his feelings for Meg but that he is not going to say anything unless he earns a comfortable home. Also, she and Mr March are not going to marry Meg so early.
- Mrs March asks Jo to keep this conversation a secret and that Meg should not find out about this. However, Jo is anxious that if Meg gets married the fun times the girls had together will cease.

# Chapter 11

Like sunshine, after a storm were the peaceful weeks which followed. The invalids improved rapidly and Mr March began to talk of returning home early in the New Year. As Christmas approached, the usual excitement permeated the house and Jo frequently convulsed the family by proposing utterly absurd ceremonies, in honour of this unusually merry Christmas.

Beth felt uncommonly well that morning. Being dressed in her mother's gift, a soft crimson merino wrapper, she was held high into the window to behold the offering of Jo and Laurie. They had done their best and conjured a comical surprise. Out in the garden stood a stately snow maiden, crowned with holly, bearing a basket of fruit and flowers in one hand, a great roll of music in the other, and a Christmas carol issuing from her lips on a pink paper streamer.

How Beth laughed when she saw it, how Laurie ran up and down to bring in the gifts, and what ridiculous speeches Jo made as she presented them.

'I'm so full of happiness, I only wish Father was here with us!' said Beth, contented as Jo carried her off to the study to rest after the excitement and to refresh herself with some of the delicious grapes.

Half an hour later, Laurie opened the parlour door and announced in a voice so treacherously joyful that everyone jumped up, 'Here's another Christmas present for the March family.'

Before she could complete her sentence, there appeared a tall man, muffled up to the eyes, leaning on the arm of another tall man, who tried to say something but couldn't. For several minutes everybody said and did the strangest things. Mr March disappeared in the embrace of four pairs of loving arms. Mrs March, held up her hand with a warning, 'Hush! Remember Beth.'

The warning came too late. Jo had put strength into the feeble limbs and Beth ran straight into her father's arms. After that, the full hearts overflowed, washing away the sorrows and misery of the past and leaving only the sweetness of the present. As the euphoria subsided, Mrs March began to thank Mr Brooke for his faithful care of her husband, who reminded her that Mr March needed rest and along with Laurie, he retired. Then the family sat together and the talking began in all earnestness.

Mr March told how he had longed to surprise them, when the fine weather came, he had been allowed by his doctor to take advantage of it, how devoted Brooke had been, and how he was altogether a most estimable and upright young man.

Mr Laurence, his grandson and Mr Brooke dined with them. They told stories, sang songs and had a thoroughly good time. As twilight gathered, the guests departed and the happy family sat together round the fire. They talked for a long time and the merry day ended with Beth playing the piano and everyone joining her in singing a beautiful hymn.

## Chapter Highlights

- Soon, both Beth and Mr March are on the road to recovery. Mr March even suggests that he might return early in the New Year. On Christmas Day, Jo is filled with excitement. Beth too feels much better and she laughs for the first time in days at Jo and Laurie's jokes.
- After much excitement and merriment, Beth is led back to the study after everyone has opened their presents. It is then that Laurie announces that there is another Christmas present.
- The next minute, a tall man enters the room leaning on the arm of John Brooke. An instant later, all four March girls have embraced Mr March with shrieks of laughter.
- After a while, when the excitement had subsided a little, Laurie and Mr Brooke take their leave. As the family sits together, Mr March tells them that he had been planning to surprise them for a while. He also tells them that John has taken good care of him all along.
- Later, Mr Laurence, Mr Brooke and Laurie dine with the Marches. When the guests leave, Beth sits at the piano and plays wonderful music which fills the hearts of her beloved family with happiness.

## Chapter 12

'Tell me if John spoke to you about this, would you cry or blush, instead of a decided no?' asked Jo.

'I'm not so silly and weak as you think. I know exactly what to say!'

Jo smiled and asked, 'Tell me what would you say?'

'Thank you, Mr Brooke, you have been very kind to all of us but I am too young to think about any engagement at present. Let's remain friends as we were.'

'Hmm, that's alright but I don't believe you'll ever say it. Even if you did, he won't be satisfied! If he goes on like the rejected lovers in books, you'll give in, rather than hurt his feelings.'

'No, I won't. I shall tell him I've made up my mind, and shall walk out of the room with dignity.'

Just then, someone gave a modest tap, opened the door with a, 'Good afternoon. I came to see how your father is and take my umbrella!' said Mr Brooke, getting a trifle confused as he looked at one telltale face to the other.

'It's very well, he's in the rack. I'll get him, and tell the umbrella that you are here.' And having mixed up her father and the umbrella, Jo slipped out of the room to give Meg a chance to make her speech. The instant she vanished, Meg began to slide toward the door, mumbling, 'I will call Mother. Pray sit down!'

'Wait, Margaret! Are you afraid of me?' said Mr Brooke,

looking so hurt that Meg thought she must have been very rude. 'Why should I be? You have been so kind to Father. I wish I knew how to thank you for it.'

'Shall I tell you how?' asked Mr Brooke, holding her small hand in his own and looking down at her with so much love in his brown eyes that her heart began to flutter.

'I won't trouble you. I only want to know if you care for me a little, Meg. I love you dearly,' added Mr Brooke tenderly. This was the moment for her speech but Meg forgot every word of it, hung her head and answered, 'I don't know. I'm too young.'

'I'll wait and in the meantime, you could learn to like me.'

As an anticlimax, Aunt March came hobbling in at this interesting minute.

She had met Laurie and hearing of Mr March's arrival, drove straight out to see him. She walked in quietly, hoping to surprise them. She did surprise two of them. Meg startled as if she had seen a ghost and Mr Brooke vanished into the study.

'Bless me, what's all this?' cried the old lady as she glanced from the pale young gentleman to the scarlet young lady.

'I've something to tell you! If you intend to marry this fellow, not one penny of my money ever goes to you. So be sensible,' remarked the old lady.

Aunt March had perfected the art of rousing the spirit of opposition in the gentlest souls especially when young and in love. Meg promptly decided that she would accept John Brooke. Meg opposed the old lady with unusual spirit.

'I shall marry whom I please, Aunt March and you can leave your money to anyone you like,' she replied, with a resolute air.

But Aunt March did not give up but started afresh, in as mild a manner as she could, 'Meg, my dear! I don't want you to spoil your whole life by making a mistake at the beginning. It's your duty to make a rich match.'

'Father and Mother don't think so. They like John though he is poor. Aunt March, my John wouldn't marry for money, any more than I would,' cried Meg indignantly, forgetting everything.

Meg stopped there, remembering all of a sudden that John might be overhearing her inconsistent remarks.

'Well, I wash my hands off the whole affair!' Slamming the door in Meg's face, Aunt March drove off in anger. Meg stood undecided when Mr Brooke appeared. 'I couldn't help hearing, Meg. Thank you for defending me, proving my worth and admitting before Aunt March that you do care for me!'

'I didn't know myself till she abused you,' began Meg.

Fifteen minutes after Aunt March's departure, Jo came softly downstairs hoping the matter with Mr Brooks had ended but she was hurt seeing him with her Meg, laughing happily.

That was too much for Jo to digest and she vanished without a word. Rushing upstairs, she startled the invalids by exclaiming, 'Oh, somebody go down quickly! John Brooke is acting strange and Meg likes it!'

Mr and Mrs March left the room with speed and casting herself upon the bed, Jo cried and told the awful news to Beth and Amy. The little girls, however, considered it a most agreeable and interesting event. This did not comfort Jo.

A great deal of talking was done in the parlour that evening and quiet Mr Brooke astonished his friends by the eloquence and spirit and finally all things for the wedding were settled.

The tea bell rang and he proudly took Meg in to supper, both looking so happy that Jo hadn't the heart to be jealous or dismal. Amy was very much impressed by John's devotion and Meg's dignity, Beth beamed at them from a distance, while Mr and Mrs March surveyed the young couple with tender satisfaction. The old room seemed to brighten up amazingly when the first romance of the family began there.

'Just then the front door banged and Laurie came prancing in, overflowing with good spirits, bearing a great bridal-looking bouquet for 'Mrs John Brooke'.

'You don't look happy Jo?' asked Laurie, following her into a corner of the parlour.

'You won't understand I've lost my dearest friend,' sighed Jo.

'You've got me, anyhow. I'm not good but I'll stand by you, Jo, all the days of my life.' And Laurie meant what he said.

'I know you will and I'm ever so much obliged. You are always a great comfort to me, Teddy,' returned Jo, gratefully shaking hands.

### Chapter Highlights

- Meg , however, learns about John's feelings for her. When Jo asks her how she will react if John asks her about his feelings for her. Meg says that she will tell him that she is too young and that they should remain friends. Jo is unconvinced.
- Just then the two sisters are interrupted by John Brooke, who has come to ask about Mr March's health. Jo excuses herself saying that she will bring him straight away. Meg says that she will fetch their mother. Seeing that she is trying to avoid him, John asks her if she is afraid of him.
- Meg says that she is grateful that he has been so kind to their father. Then, John confesses his love for Meg and her only reply is that she is too young.
- Aunt March chooses this particular moment to make an entrance. She states that Meg should not marry a poor man and if she does, she is not going to get one penny

from her. Meg opposes her, saying that she will marry who she wants to and that she can do what she likes with her money.

- Nothing deters Aunt March and she starts insulting John. Meg says that her John will not marry for money. Angry, Aunt March slams the door and leaves.
- John Brooke comes forward and says that he didn't know that Meg cared for him. She confesses that she didn't know herself until her aunt had started abusing him.
- After a while, Jo comes to find out if the matter with John Brooke is ended but is hurt to see both of them laughing. Without a word, she tells her parents that John Brooke is sitting with Meg. When Beth and Amy learn of it, the girls are delighted.
- Mr and Mrs March spend a lot of time with Meg and John in the parlour and the discussion ends when all the things about the wedding are settled.
- Jo is sad as she is losing her best friend. Laurie comforts her saying that she still has him for his friend.

# Part II

## Chapter 13

The three years have brought but few changes to the quiet family. The war is over and Mr March safely at home, busy with his books and the small parish which found in him a minister by nature as by grace.

To outsiders the five energetic women seemed to rule the house and so they did in many things but the quiet scholar, sitting among his books, was still the head of the family, the household conscience, anchor, and comforter.

The girls gave their hearts into their mother's keeping, their souls into their father's, and to both parents, who lived and laboured so faithfully for them; they gave a love that grew with them and bound them tenderly together by the sweetest tie which blesses life and outlives death.

Mrs March is as brisk and cheery, though a bit grey. She is so absorbed in Meg's affairs. John Brooke did his duty, preparing for business and earning a home for Meg. With the good sense and sturdy independence that characterized him, he refused Mr Laurence's more generous offers and accepted the place of a bookkeeper.

Meg had spent the time in growing wise in housewifely arts and prettier than ever, for love is a great beautifier. Jo never went back to Aunt March, for the old lady took such a fancy to Amy that she bribed her with drawing lessons from one of the best teachers. Jo meantime devoted herself to literature and Beth, who remained delicate long after the fever, remained happy and busy with the quiet duties she loved. She was everyone's friend and an angel in the house!

As long as The Spread Eagle paid her a dollar a column for her 'rubbish', as she called it, Jo felt herself a woman of means and spun her little romances diligently.

Laurie, having dutifully gone to college to please his grandfather, was now getting through it in the easiest possible manner. 'Dovecote' was the name of the little brown house Mr Brooke had prepared for Meg. Laurie had christened it, saying it was highly appropriate to the gentle lovers who 'went on together like a pair of turtledoves.' It was a tiny house, with a little garden behind and a lawn about as big as a pocket handkerchief in the front. The inside was altogether charming and the happy bride saw no fault from garret to cellar.

'Are you satisfied? Does it seem like home and do you feel as if you should be happy here?' asked Mrs March, as she and her daughter went through the new kingdom arm in arm, more tenderly than ever.

'Yes, Mother, perfectly satisfied, thanks to you all!' she added.

### Chapter Highlights

- Three years have passed since the marriage between Meg and John Brooke has been decided. The war is over and Mr March is back home and is a minister of a small parish.
- The five women rule the house and Mr March is always there to support and guide them. John Brooke has been working hard to have a home for Meg and has started working as a bookkeeper.

- Aunt March takes fancy to Amy and she stays with her. Jo has devoted herself to literature and her stories often get published now, Meg has been learning the duties of a wife and Beth, weakened by the fever, enjoys the duties she loves. Laurie, meanwhile, has been attending college according to the wishes of his grandfather.
- 'Dovecote' is the house that John Brooke prepares for Meg. It is a small house with a little garden behind it and a lawn in the front.
- Mrs March, along with her daughters, examines the house. Meg loves it.

# Chapter 14

The June roses were awake bright and early on that morning, all over the porch, rejoicing with all their hearts in the cloudless sunshine as if offering their tribute of beauty and fragrance to the gentle mistress who had loved and tended them so long.

Meg looked very like a rose herself, for all that was best and sweetest in heart and soul seemed to bloom into her face that day. She did not want silk, lace, nor orange flowers as she said, 'I don't want a fashionable wedding, but only those about me whom I love and with them I wish to be my familiar self.'

She made her wedding gown herself, sewing into it the tender hopes and innocent romances of a girlish heart. Her sisters braided up her pretty hair and the only ornaments she wore were the lilies of the valley, which 'her John' liked best of all the flowers.

The three years had wrought subtle changes in the countenance of the girls and all were looking their best. Jo's angles are softened considerably; she has learnt to carry herself with ease, if not grace. The curly crop has lengthened into a thick coil. There was a fresh colour in her brown cheeks, a soft shine in her eyes and she spoke only gentle words. Beth has grown slender, pale, and quieter than ever. The beautiful, kind eyes are larger, and in them lay a sad expression, a shadow of pain.

Amy is considered 'the flower of the family', for at sixteen she has the air and bearing of a full-grown woman, possessed of immense grace. Her wonderfully fair complexion, keen blue eyes, and curls more golden and abundant than ever.

All three wore suits of thin silver grey with blush roses in hair and bosom and all three looked just what they were, fresh-faced, happy-hearted girls.

There were to be no ceremonious performances, everything was to be as natural and homelike as possible, so when Aunt March arrived, she was scandalized to see the bride running to welcome and lead her in, to find the bridegroom fastening up a garland that had fallen.

A crash, a cry, and a laugh from Laurie, accompanied by the indecorous exclamation, "Jo's upset the cake again!" caused a momentary flurry. There was no bridal procession but a sudden silence fell upon the room as Mr March and the young couple took their places under the green arch. Mother and sisters gathered close, as if reluctant to give Meg up. The fatherly voice broke more than once, which only seemed to make the service more beautiful and solemn. The bridegroom's hand trembled visibly, and no one heard his replies. But Meg looked straight up in her husband's eyes and said, 'I will!' with such tender trust in her own face and voice that her mother's heart rejoiced and Aunt March sniffed audibly.

During the next fifteen minutes, everyone surrounded and blessed the couple. There was no display of gifts, for they were already in the little house, nor was there an elaborate breakfast, but a plentiful lunch of cake and fruit, dressed with flowers.

After lunch, Meg and John stood together in the middle of the grass plot, when Laurie was seized with an inspiration which put the finishing touch to this unfashionable wedding.

'All the married people hold hands and dance round the new-wedded couple, as the Germans do, while we bachelors and spinsters prance in pairs outside!' cried Laurie, promenading down the path with Amy, with such infectious spirit and skill that everyone else followed their example without a murmur. As the ball was set to close, people began to go.

'I wish you well, my dear, I heartily wish you well,' said Aunt March to Meg, adding to the bridegroom, 'You've got a treasure, young man, see that you deserve it.'

The little house was not far away and the only bridal journey Meg had was the quiet walk with John from the old home to the new. Everyone gathered about her to say 'goodbye' tenderly.

'Don't feel that I am separated from you or that I love you any the less for loving John so much,' she said, clinging to her mother. They stood watching her, with faces full of love and hope and tender pride as she walked away, leaning on her husband's arm.

### Chapter Highlights

- It is Meg's wedding day. She does not want a fashionable wedding but insists that her family should be around.
- Three years have brought subtle changes in the girls. Jo has learnt to carry herself with ease if not grace. Beth has grown slender and pale and there is a shadow of pain in her eyes. Amy, at sixteen, has grown up to be a lady.
- The wedding is a low-key affair. The bride is welcoming the guests while the groom is making sure that no decoration is amiss.
- The ceremony itself is quiet. The bridegroom is nervous but the bride is confident about the journey she is embarking on.
- After the wedding, everyone blesses the new couple and soon, they go quietly to their new home.

# Chapter 15

Fortune suddenly smiled upon Jo and a small sum for her writing started coming to her. Every few weeks she would shut herself up in her room, put on her scribbling suit and absorb herself completely in writing her novel.

Once a while she was just recovering from one of these attacks, when she was prevailed upon to escort Miss Crocker to a lecture and in return, was rewarded with a new idea.

They reached early and Jo amused herself by examining the faces of the people who occupied the seat with them. On her right, was a studious looking lad absorbed in a tabloid. The boy noticed Jo was also attempting to read it, with her head cocked to one side. Pausing to turn the page, he with boyish good nature, offered half his paper, asking, 'Want to read it? That's a first-rate story.'

Jo accepted it, with a smile and got busy reading the tabloid.

'Prime, isn't it?' asked the boy, as her eye went down the last paragraph of her portion.

'I guess you and I could do a better job, if we tried,' returned Jo, amused at his admiration of the trash.

By now the lecture began but Jo was covertly taking down the address of the paper and boldly resolving to try for the hundred-dollar prize offered in its columns for a sensational story. By the time the lecture ended, she had built up a splendid plot for herself.

She told no one at home about her plan but fell to work

right away. Jo had never tried this style before. Her experience and miscellaneous reading were of service now, for they gave her some idea of dramatic effect and supplied the plot and language.

The manuscript was privately dispatched. Six weeks is a long time to wait and a still longer time for a girl to keep a secret but Jo did both. When she was just beginning to give up, a letter arrived which almost took her breath away, for on opening it, a cheque for a hundred dollars fell into her lap.

For a minute she stared at it and then read the letter, with tears welling in her eyes. She electrified the family by appearing before them with the letter in one hand, the cheque in the other, announcing that she had won the prize. There was great celebration and when the story came, everyone read and praised it. Her father told her that the language was good, the romance fresh but he added in his unworldly way, 'You can do better than this, Jo. Aim at the highest, and never mind the money.'

'I think the money is the best part of it. What will you do with such a fortune?' asked Amy.

'Send Beth and Mother to the seaside for a month or two,' answered Jo promptly.

To the seaside they went and though Beth didn't come home as plump and rosy as was desired, she was much better, while Mrs March declared she felt ten years younger. So Jo was satisfied with the investment of her prize money and fell to work with a cheery spirit, bent on earning more of those delightful cheques. She did earn several that year, for by the magic of a pen, her 'rubbish' turned into comforts for them all.

Her stories found a market. Encouraged, by this fact, she resolved to make a bold stroke for fame and fortune. Having copied her novel for the fourth time, read it to all her confidential friends, and submitted it with fear and trepidation, to three publishers, who agreed to publish it on the condition that she would cut it down by one third which meant omitting all those parts which she particularly admired.

The novel was finally printed. Jo got three hundred dollars for it and plenty of praise and blame. She was in a state of bewilderment from which she took some time to recover.

## Chapter Highlights

- In time, Jo's writings start appearing in the newspapers. Once she gets an idea for her new story when she visits a lecture. It is also there that she learns about a contest where the winner will get a hundred dollar prize for writing a sensational story.
- Once at home, Jo busies herself in writing a story and dispatches it without telling anyone about it. Six weeks pass by before the result is out. One day, a letter comes with a cheque for hundred dollars in it.
- With the letter in one hand and the cheque in the other, she goes to her family and tells them how she has won the contest and the prize. A great celebration takes place.
- Later, Jo declares that she wants Beth and Mother to go to the seaside for a month using the prize money. On their return Beth certainly looks better and Mrs March says that she feels ten years younger.
- Jo wins more cheques for her stories and she is happy, though her father says that she can write better.
- Finally, Jo has her novel published and gets three hundred dollars for it. She is in a state of bewilderment from which she takes some time to recover.

# Chapter 16

Like most young wives, Meg began her married life with the determination to be a model housekeeper. John should find home a paradise; he should always see a smiling face, should have a sumptuous fare every day and never know the loss of a button. She brought lots of love, energy, and cheerfulness to the work, despite few obstacles. As a result, she was too tired, sometimes, even to smile. John grew dyspeptic due to all the dainty dishes and plainly asked for plain fare.

They were very happy, even after they discovered that they couldn't live on love alone. John did not find Meg's beauty diminished, though she beamed at him from behind the familiar coffee pot. Nor did Meg miss the romance in the daily parting, when her husband followed up his kiss with the tender enquiry, 'Shall I send some veal or mutton for dinner, darling?'

The little house soon became a home and the young couple felt that it was a change for the better. So the year rolled round and at midsummer there came to Meg a new experience, the deepest and tenderest of a woman's life. When Laurie came sneaking into the kitchen of the Dovecote one Saturday, he was received by Hannah.

'How's the little mamma? Where is everybody? Why didn't you tell me before I came home?' began Laurie in a loud whisper.

'Happy as a queen! The family is upstairs. We didn't want

hurricanes round. Now you go into the parlour and I'll get them down to you,' and Hannah and vanished, chuckling ecstatically.

Soon Jo came down, proudly holding a flannel bundle. Her face was very sober but her eyes twinkled.

'Shut your eyes and hold out your arms,' she ordered.

Laurie implored, 'No, thank you. I'd rather not. I shall drop the baby.'

'Then you shan't see your nephew,' said Jo decidedly, turning as if to go.

'I will! Only you must be responsible for damages.' And obeying orders, Laurie heroically shut his eyes while something was put into his arms. A peal of laughter from Jo, Amy, Mrs March, Hannah and John caused him to open them the next minute, to find himself invested with two babies instead of one.

No wonder they laughed at the expression on his face, as he stood and stared wildly from the unconscious innocents to the hilarious spectators with such dismay that Jo sat down on the floor, in fits of laughter.

'Twins, by Jove!' was all he said for a minute, then turning to the women with an appealing look that was comically piteous, he added, 'Somebody hold them! I'm going to laugh and I shall drop them.'

Jo rescued the babies, and marched up and down, with one on each arm.

'Isn't it simply delightful? Are they boys? What are you going to name them? Let's have another look!' replied Laurie.

'Boy and girl. Aren't they beauties?' said the proud papa, beaming with undisguised joy.

'Most remarkable children I ever saw. Which is which?' asked Laurie examining the infants.

'Amy put a blue ribbon on the boy and a pink on the girl, French fashion, so you can always tell. Besides, one has blue eyes and one brown. Kiss them, Uncle Teddy,' said wicked Jo.

'Name him Demijohn, and call her Daisy,' said Laurie.

'Daisy and Demi, just the right names! I knew Teddy would do it,' cried Jo clapping her hands.

## Chapter Highlights

- Meg begins her married life with a determination to be a model housekeeper. She does everything with lots of love, happiness and energy. The young couple is happy. In no time, the house becomes a home.
- A year passes by and the young couple are in for a new experience.
- One day, Laurie sneaks into Dovecote, meets Hannah and asks her how the young mother is doing. She asks him to wait in the parlour while she calls the family down.
- Soon, Jo comes down holding a flannel bundle and asks Laurie to close his eyes and hold out his arms.
- After some protest, he does as he is instructed. Something is placed in his arms and he opens his eyes only when he hears laughter. Everyone is in the parlour and they are amused.
- Laurie looks down at the arms and sees that he is holding not one but two babies. Seeing his expression, everyone laughs. Jo soon rescues him and holds the babies one in each arm.
- The babies are names Daisy and Demijohn. The family is delighted and are unable to disguise their happiness.

## Chapter 17

'Let's go home and never mind Aunt March today. We can run down there any time!'

'Speak for yourself! Aunt March likes our making a formal call. It's a little thing to do, but it gives her pleasure and it will not hurt you in any way!' spoke Amy curtly.

'What a good girl you are, Amy! I wish it was as easy for me to do little things to please people as it is for you.' said Jo.

Amy smiled and was mollified at once, saying with a maternal air, 'Women should learn to be agreeable, particularly poor ones! Now compose yourself and don't scandalize aunt with your strange ideas.'

'I'll try not to, but I'm always possessed to burst out with some particularly blunt speech or revolutionary sentiment before her. I can't help it.'

They found Aunt Carrol with the old lady, both absorbed in some very interesting subject, but they became quiet as the girls came in, which betrayed that they had been talking about their nieces. Jo was not in a good humour and the perverse fit returned but Amy was courteous and pleased everybody. Her amiable spirit was felt at once and both aunts began talking to her affectionately, saying emphatically, 'That child improves every day.'

'Do you speak French, dear?' asked Mrs Carrol, laying a hand on Amy's.

'Pretty well, thanks to Aunt March, who lets Esther talk to me as often as I like,' replied Amy, with a grateful look, which caused the old lady to smile affably.

Aunt March said to Amy, 'You are quite strong and well now, dear, I believe? Eyes don't trouble you any more, do they?'

'Not at all, thank you, Aunt! I'm very well, and mean to do great things next winter, so that I may be ready for Rome, whenever that joyful time arrives.'

'Good girl! You deserve to go, and I'm sure you will soon,' said Aunt March, with an approving look.

After a while, when the girls departed leaving behind them the impression of shadow and sunshine, Aunt March said, 'You'd better do it, Mary. I'll supply the money.'

Aunt Carrol replied decidedly, 'I certainly will, if her parents' consent.'

A week later, Amy got her reward. 'Aunt Carrol is going abroad next month and wants...'

'Me to go with her!' burst in Jo, flying out of her chair in an uncontrollable rapture.

'No, not you, dear, it's Amy.'

'Oh, Mother! She's too young, it's my turn first. I've wanted it so long. It would do me so much good. I must go!'

'I'm afraid it's partly your own fault, dear. When Aunt spoke to me the other day, she regretted your blunt manners and too independent a spirit.'

'Oh, my abominable tongue! Why can't I learn to control it?' groaned Jo. Mrs March said sorrowfully, 'I wish you could have gone but there is no way out; so bear it cheerfully and don't sadden Amy's pleasure!'

There was not much time for preparation and everyone was in a tizzy. Jo bore up very well but finally retired to the garret and cried her heart out. Amy likewise bore up stoutly till the steamer sailed.

## Chapter Highlights

- After some time, Jo and Amy are going to meet Aunt March. Jo compliments Amy saying that she is graceful and always ready to do anything to please people. Amy replies that poor girls should learn to be agreeable.
- When the girls reach Aunt March's house, they find her sitting with Aunt Carrol. Seeing them, the two old ladies cease their conversation. It is evident that they were talking about their nieces.
- Both the aunts find Amy very agreeable and charming while Jo's blunt manners are disliked by them.
- A week later, they receive a message from Aunt Carrol where she wants Amy to accompany her on her trip abroad next month. Jo is devastated. She had counted on her aunt to take her on this trip. Marmee reminds Jo that it is partly her own fault. She should not have shown her independent spirit to her aunt.
- Preparations for Amy's journey begin at once. A week later, she is on a steamer with Aunt Carrol.

# Chapter 18

While Amy kept the family posted about her adventures, Mrs March was upset about the quiet little one at home.

'Jo, I'm worried about Beth.'

'Why, Mother, doesn't she seem better since the babies came.'

'It's not her health but her spirits. There is something on her mind which worries me. She sits all by herself, doesn't talk to her father as she used to. The other day, I found her crying over the babies. Her songs are always sad and there is a look in her face that I don't understand and it worries me.'

'Have you talked to her about it?'

'I have tried once or twice but she either evades my questions or looks so distressed that I stop. I leave Beth in your hands, for she will open her tender little heart to her Jo sooner than to anyone else. Be very kind, and don't let her think anyone watches or talks about her.'

Jo stitched away, with a wise nod which set her mother's heart at rest. She was busy writing one day, with Beth sitting next to her. As she scribbled, she kept her eye on her sister, who seemed unusually quiet. Sitting at the window, Beth frequently leaned her head upon her hand, in a dejected attitude.

Suddenly someone passed below, whistling and a voice called out, 'Hi Serene! Coming in, tonight.'

Beth leaned forward, smiled and fondly watched the passerby till his quick tramp died away, then said softly as if to herself, 'How strong, well and happy that dear boy looks!'

Jo saw that the bright colour faded as quickly as it came, the smile vanished and a tear lay shining on the window ledge. 'Mercy me, Beth loves Laurie!' she said, sitting down in her own room, pale with the shock of the discovery which she had made. 'I would never have dreamt of such a thing. What will Mother say? What if he shouldn't love her! I'll make him love her!' she promised to herself.

In the evening she made some new observations, which only confirmed her suspicion. Though Laurie was in the habit of flirting with Amy and joking with Jo, his manner to Beth had always been peculiarly kind and gentle. Therefore, no one imagined that he cared more for her than for the others. Indeed, a general impression had prevailed in the family of late that 'our boy' was getting fonder than ever of Jo, who, however, wouldn't hear a word of this nonsense.

When Laurie first went to college, he fell in love about once a month, but these small flames were brief, did no damage and amused Jo, which were confided to her in their weekly conferences. Soon there came a time when Laurie ceased to worship at many shrines, hinted darkly at one all-absorbing passion. Then he avoided the tender subject altogether and wrote philosophical notes to Jo.

Things were in this state when the grand discovery was made and Jo watched Laurie that night as she had never done before. If she had not got the new idea into her head, she would have seen nothing unusual in the fact that Beth was very quiet and Laurie very kind to her. That evening Jo fancied that Beth's eyes rested on Laurie's lively face with peculiar pleasure.

'Come, Jo, don't be so harsh! After studying himself to a skeleton all through the week, a fellow deserves some pampering and ought to get it.'

'Beth will pamper you. I'm busy.'

'No, she's not to be bothered with me, unless you've suddenly started to hate your boy!'

Jo knew that 'young Laurence' was regarded as the most eligible boy by worldly mamas, was much smiled upon by their daughters and flattered enough by ladies of all ages, so she watched him rather jealously, fearing he would be spoilt and rejoiced that he still believed in modest girls.

Jo lay long awake that night and just when she was dropping off, the sound of a stifled sob made her fly to Beth's bedside, with the anxious inquiry, 'What is it, dear?'

'I thought you were asleep,' sobbed Beth.

'Is it the old pain, my precious?'

'No, it's a new one but I can bear it,' replied Beth holding back her tears.

'Tell me all about it, and let me cure it!'

'You can't, there is no cure,' and clinging to her sister, she cried so despairingly that Jo was frightened.

'Does anything trouble you, dear?'

'Yes!'

'Wouldn't it comfort you to tell me what it is?'

'Not yet.'

'Then I won't ask, but remember dear that Mother and Jo are always ready to hear and help you, if they can.'

◆

Next morning, Jo had made up her mind. She had been pondering over a project for some days, and finally, she confided it to her mother.

'Marmee,' she began. 'I want to go away somewhere this winter for a change.'

'Why, Jo?' and her mother looked up quickly.

'I feel restless and am keen to see, do and learn more. I brood too much over my own small affairs. I need stirring up.'

'Where will you hop?'

'To New York. I had a bright idea yesterday. Mrs Kirke had written to you for some respectable young person to teach her children to read and sew. It's rather hard to find just the thing but I think I should suit, if I tried.'

Mrs March looked surprised, but not displeased.

'What about your writing?'

'I shall see and hear new things, get new ideas and I shall bring home quantities of material for my writing.'

'I have no doubt of it, but are these your only reasons for this sudden fancy?'

Jo looked up and down. Then, with sudden colour in her cheeks, she said, 'I'm afraid Laurie is getting too fond of me.'

'Then you don't care for him in the way it is evident he begins to care for you?' and Mrs March looked anxious.

'No, mother! I love the dear boy, as I always have and am immensely proud of him but as for anything more, it's out of the question.'

'I'm glad of that, Jo.'

'Why?'

'Because, I don't think you are suited to one another. As friends you are very happy and your frequent quarrels soon blow over, but I fear you would both rebel if you were mated for life. You are too much alike and too fond of freedom, not to mention hot tempers and strong wills, to get on happily together, in a relation which needs infinite patience and forbearance, as well as love.'

'That's just the feeling I had, though I couldn't express it. I'm glad you think he is only beginning to care for me. It would trouble me sadly to make him unhappy, for I couldn't fall in love with the dear old fellow merely out of gratitude, could I? Let us say nothing about it to Laurie till the plan is settled, then I'll run away before he can collect his wits.'

The plan was talked over in a family council and agreed upon. Mrs Kirke gladly accepted Jo and promised to make a pleasant home for her. Jo liked the prospect and was eager to leave, for the home nest was growing too narrow for her restless and adventurous spirit.

When Laurie said goodbye, he whispered significantly, 'It won't do a bit of good, Jo. My eye is on you, so mind what you do or I'll come and bring you home.'

◆

Dear Marmee and Beth, I've got heaps to tell! Mrs Kirke welcomed me so kindly I felt at home at once. She gave me a cute little sky parlour, with a stove and a nice table in a sunny window, so I can sit here and write whenever I like. The nursery, where I am to teach and sew, is a pleasant room next to Mrs Kirke's private parlour and the two little girls are pretty children, rather spoilt but they started liking me after I narrated a story to them and I've no doubt I shall make a model governess.

'Dear, make yourself at home,' said Mrs Kirke in her motherly way, 'My rooms are always open to you and your own shall be as comfortable as I can make it. Your evenings are always free.'

I'm glad Laurie seems so happy and I am sure Beth manages him better than I did. Do your best, Beth, only don't make a saint of him. I had a very happy New Year, though I missed you all. I am cheerful all the time now, work with a will, and take more interest in other people than I used to, which is satisfactory.

Jo

## Chapter Highlights

- Amy keeps her family posted about her adventures. However, Mrs March is worried about Beth. She has become quieter and there is something on her mind which she is keeping to herself. She asks Jo to talk to Beth.
- One day, while Jo is writing another story, Beth comes and sits beside the window. Jo observes Beth from time to time and realizes that her sister has gone quiet and that she is dispirited.
- Suddenly, someone passes by the window and greets an acquaintance. Beth smiles seeing him and remarks how healthy that boy is. The next moment, the smile vanishes. Jo has a sudden realization that Beth is in love with Laurie.
- Jo knows that though Laurie flirts with Amy and jokes with her, he is particularly kind to Beth.
- That evening, when Laurie comes over, Jo observes that Beth is very quiet and Laurie compassionate towards her.
- Later that night, Jo is lying in her bed thinking when she hears a sob. At once, she goes to Beth.
- Jo asks Beth what is hurting her but she says that she will tell her about it when it is time. Jo assures Beth that she can confide when she wants in either Mother or herself.
- Next day, Jo confides in her mother about a project she has been thinking about for some time. She says that she wants to go to New York for some time to learn and explore new things.
- Marmee is surprised but not displeased. Jo even suggests, referring to the telegram that Marmee had received the day before, where Mrs Kirke has asked for a teacher for her daughters. Jo wants to take the place. She also says

that this adventure will also help her to get new ideas for her stories.

- Marmee asks Jo if this is the only reason that she wants to go away. Jo confesses that Laurie is getting too fond of her. She adds that she cannot reciprocate his feelings more than being friends. Mrs March supports her and they decide that Laurie should know nothing about it.
- The March family too agrees with the plan. Mrs Kirke is happy to have Jo. When the time comes to say goodbye, Laurie whispers to Jo that going away will not do her any good.
- Some time passes and Jo sends a letter saying that she has been welcomed wholeheartedly by Mrs Kirke and feels quite at home. She has a comfortable room to stay in and Mrs Kirke's girls have become fond of her. She wants Beth to look after herself.

# Chapter 19

Though very busy with the daily work and happy in the new atmosphere, Jo still found time for literary labours. She saw that money conferred power and she resolved to have it, not to be used for herself alone, but for those whom she loved more than life. She dreamt of filling home with comforts, giving Beth everything she wanted.

The prize-story experience had seemed to open the way but the novel disaster had left her in a dilemma, for public opinion is such a giant that she was disheartened.

She took to writing sensation stories, for people read rubbish. She told no one, but concocted a 'thrilling tale' and boldly carried it to Mr Dashwood, the editor of the Weekly Volcano. She dressed herself well and bravely climbed two flights of dark stairs. She found herself in a room clouded by cigar smoke and with three gentlemen.

Jo hesitated on the threshold, murmuring, 'Excuse me, I was looking for the Weekly Volcano office. I wished to see Mr Dashwood.'

Jo held her manuscript and blushingly, blundered out fragments of the little speech carefully prepared for the occasion, 'A friend of mine has asked me to bring this story as an experiment and would like your opinion. She would be glad to write more if this suits you.'

Mr Dashwood took the manuscript and was casting critical glances up and down the neat pages.

'Not the first attempt, I take it?' he spoke, observing that the pages were numbered, covered only on one side.

'No, sir. She has some experience and has even won a prize for a tale.'

'Oh, did she?' and Mr Dashwood gave Jo a quick look, which seemed to take note of everything she had on. 'Well, you can leave it, if you like. We'll tell you by next week.'

Now, Jo did not wish to leave it but there was nothing for her to do but to bow and walk away. Half resolving never to return, she went back and worked off her irritation by stitching pinafores vigorously and in an hour or two, was cool enough to laugh over the scene and wait for next week.

When she went the next week, Mr Dashwood was alone, which put her at ease. He was not so heavily smoking his cigar to forget his manners and so the second meeting was much more comfortable than the first.

'We'll take this, if you don't object to a few alterations. It's too long, but omitting the passages I've marked will make it just the right length,' he said, in a businesslike tone.

Jo hardly recognized her own manuscript, so crumpled and underscored were its pages. She felt like a parent who was being asked to cut off her baby's legs so that it fits into a new cradle. She was surprised to find that all the moral reflections, which she had carefully put in, had been scored out.

'Sir, I thought every story should have some moral, so I took care to have a few of my sinners repent.'

Mr Dashwood's editorial gravity relaxed into a smile, for Jo had forgotten her 'friend', and spoken as only an author could.

'People want to be amused, not preached at! Morals don't sell nowadays,' was Mr Dashwood's affable reply.

'What compensation,' stuttered Jo, not exactly knowing how to express herself.

'Oh, yes, well, we give from twenty-five to thirty for this sort of work and pay when it's published,' returned Mr Dashwood, as if that point had escaped him.

'Very well, you can have it,' said Jo, handing back the story with satisfaction, for after the dollar-a- column work, twenty-five seemed really good.

'Shall I tell my friend you will take another if she has one better than this?' asked Jo, emboldened by her success.

'Well, we'll look at it but can't promise to take it. Tell her to make it short and spicy and not at all moralistic. What name would your friend like to put on it?' he asked in a careless tone.

'None at all, if you please, she doesn't wish her name to appear and so far has no pen name,' said Jo, blushing in spite of herself.

'Alright! The tale will be out next week. Will you call for the money, or shall I send it?' asked Mr Dashwood, who felt a natural desire to know who his new contributor might be.'

'I'll call. Good day, sir.'

Following Mr Dashwood's directions, Jo rashly took a plunge into the frothy sea of sensational literature. Like most young scribblers, she went abroad for her characters and scenery and Mr Dashwood graciously permitted her to fill his columns at the lowest prices.

She soon became interested in her work, for her purse grew stout. Her dream to take Beth to the mountains next summer, seemed to materialize. One thing disturbed her: She did not tell her family.

She had a feeling that Father and Mother would not approve of her flippant writing. It was easy to keep her secret, for no name appeared with her stories.

Mr Dashwood had of course found it out very soon, but

preferred to remain dumb.

Mr Dashwood only accepted thrilling tales for which harrowing up the souls of the readers, history and romance, land and sea, science and art, police records and lunatic asylums, had to be ransacked.

While endowing her imaginary heroes with every perfection under the sun, Jo was discovering a live hero, who interested her in spite of many human imperfections. Mr Bhaer, in one of their conversations, had advised her to study simple, true, and lovely characters, wherever she found them, as good training for a writer. Jo took him at his word.

Why everybody liked the professor puzzled Jo, at first. He was neither rich, great, young, handsome nor was he in no respect fascinating, imposing, or brilliant. Yet he was very attractive and people seemed to gather about him as naturally as about a warm hearth. He was poor, yet always appeared to be giving something away; a stranger, yet everyone was his friend. Jo often watched him, trying to discover the charm and finally decided that it was benevolence which worked the miracle.

Jo valued goodness highly but she also possessed the most feminine respect for intellect. She began to see that character is a better possession than money, rank, intellect or beauty.

She concluded that her friend Friedrich Bhaer was not only good but great. This belief strengthened daily. She valued his esteem, she coveted his respect, she wanted to be worthy of his friendship.

Jo's dear friend had subtly hinted that the trash that was printed in journals and newspapers was corrupting young minds and was worse than children playing with gunpowder. This made Jo put all her trash into the fireplace and give up writing sensational stories.

Then she tried writing a child's story, which she could easily have sold had she not been such a mercenary. Finally, she packed her inkstand and decided to wait for a while. While these internal revolutions were going on, Jo sometimes looked serious and at other times, sad. No one observed it but Professor Bhaer and he did it so quietly that Jo did not know that he was watching.

He knew that she had given up writing. He helped her in many ways, proving himself a true friend and Jo was happy, for while her pen lay idle, she was learning other lessons besides German and laying a foundation for the sensational story of her own life.

It was a pleasant winter and a long one, for she did not leave Mrs Kirke till June. Everyone seemed sorry when she departed.

She bade them all goodbye and when his turn came, she said warmly, 'I am sure sir, you won't forget to come and see us, when you travel our way, will you? I'll never forgive you if you do, for I want them all to meet my friend.'

'Shall I come?' he asked, looking down at her with an eager expression which she did not see.

'Yes, come next month. Laurie graduates then and you'd enjoy commencement as something new.'

She involuntarily began to blush and the more she tried not to, the redder she grew. She hoped that the professor did not see it but he did and he said, 'I fear I shall not be able to take out time for that but I wish your friend success and you all happiness. God bless you!'

And with that, he shook hands warmly and went away. Early next morning, he was at the station to see Jo off and she began her solitary journey with the pleasant memory of a familiar face smiling its farewell, a bunch of violets to keep her company and best of all, the happy thought, 'I've made a friend worth having and I'll try to keep him all my life.'

## Chapter Highlights

- Though busy with teaching her pupils, Jo still finds time for her literary pursuits. She realizes that money gives you power and she meant to have it. But she wanted to fill her home with comforts using it. She goes back to writing her sensational stories.
- Once she writes a thrilling story and goes to meet Mr Dashwood, editor of weekly magazine with her manuscript.
- The editor treats her coldly but observes that it is not the first attempt at writing and asks her to come back after a week.
- A week later Jo returns to the editor and learns that her story will be accepted for publication if she agrees to remove the moral angle. As she is being paid a good amount of money, Jo agrees. She asks if she can send another one and the editor says that she can but there is no guarantee that all her stories will be published.
- So, Jo becomes a regular contributor of sensational stories to the magazine, though these are published anonymously. Gradually, she has enough money to take Beth to the mountains. However, she has a feeling that her parents will not approve of these stories.
- While Jo is busy writing about people who are perfect, she meets Mr Bhaer, a language instructor in the city. He advises her to read about simple characters, and she follows it to the hilt.
- Jo often wonders about the charm that surrounds the professor. He is neither rich nor young yet people gather around him. She realizes that he, Professor Friedrich

Bhaer, is benevolent and that is a character trait she values highly. She is so influenced by his words when he says that the sensational stories in the newspapers are corrupting the younger generation that she stops writing them.

- She tries writing stories for children but the moral aspect has no market for them. She gives up writing for a while and is often sad. Professor Bhaer sees it. He helps her learn new things and lays a foundation for the sensational story of her life.
- In June, after one full year in New York, Jo decides to return home. When she says goodbye to Professor Bhaer, she invites him to come home if he is going that way.

## Chapter 20

Whatever his motive might have been, Laurie studied well and graduated with honour. They were all there—his proud grandfather, Mr and Mrs March, John and Meg, Jo and Beth, and everyone exulted over him with the sincere admiration.

'I shall be home early tomorrow. You'll come and meet me as usual, girls?' Laurie said, as he put the sisters into the carriage. Though he said 'girls' he meant Jo. She did not have the heart to refuse him anything and answered warmly, 'I'll come, Teddy, rain or shine.'

Laurie thanked her with a look that made her panic, 'Oh, dear! I know what he'll say! What shall I do?'

The long evening and morning work somewhat allayed her fears and she set forth at the appointed time. However, when she saw the familiar figure looming in the distance, she had a strong desire to run away.

She always used to hold his hand when they met but now she did not and he did not complain, which was a bad sign. He talked on rapidly about all sorts of faraway subjects, till they turned from the road into the little path that led homeward through the grove. Then he walked more slowly, suddenly lost his fine flow of language. To fill in the odd spell of silence, Jo said hastily, 'Now you must take a good long holiday!'

'I intend to.'

Something in his resolute tone made Jo look up to find him looking down at her with an expression that assured her the dreaded moment had come.

She put out her hand with an imploring, 'No, Teddy. Please don't!'

'I will, and you must hear me. It's no use, Jo, we've got to and the sooner the better for both of us,' he answered, getting flushed and excited all at once.

Laurie's voice would get choky now and then, in spite of his manly efforts to keep it steady, 'I've loved you ever since I've known you, Jo; couldn't help it, you've been so good to me. I've tried to show it but you wouldn't let me. Now I want you to hear me and give me an answer, for I can't go on like this any longer.'

'I wanted to save you this. I thought you'd understand,' began Jo, finding it much harder than she expected.

'I know you did but the girls are so queer you never know what they mean. They say no when they mean yes, and drive a man out of his wits,' replied Laurie.

'I don't. I never wanted you to go through this so I went away to keep you from it if I could.'

'I thought so as much but it served no purpose. I only loved you all the more and I worked hard to please you. I waited and never complained, for I hoped you'd love me.' His voice choked and he couldn't control it.

'No, you are too good for me and I'm very proud and fond of you. I don't know why I can't love you as you want me to. I've tried but I can't change the feeling and it would be a lie to say I do when I don't.'

'You really mean it, Jo?'

He stopped short and caught both her hands as he put his question with a look that she did not soon forget.

'Really, I do mean it, dear.'

Laurie dropped her hands and simply rested his head on the mossy post and stood so still that Jo was frightened.

'Oh, Teddy, I'm sorry, I could kill myself if it would do any good!' cried Jo and softly patted his shoulder, remembering the time when he had comforted her so long ago.

'Don't tell me Jo that you love that devilish professor you were always writing about. If you do, I shall do something desperate,' he said, clenching his fists with an angry glare in his eyes.

Jo wanted to laugh but restrained herself and said warmly, 'Don't swear, Teddy! He isn't bad. He is good, kind and the best friend I've got, after you. I haven't the least idea of loving him or anybody else.'

'But you will after a while and then what will become of me?'

'You'll love someone else too,' like a sensible boy and forget all this!'

'I can't love anyone else and I'll never forget you, Jo, Never!' he replied.

'You'll get over this after a while and find some lovely accomplished girl, who will adore you and make a fine mistress for your house. I don't like elegant society but you do and both of us will be unhappy!'

'Anything more?' asked Laurie, finding it hard to be patient.

'Nothing more, except that I don't believe I shall ever marry. I'm happy as I am and love my liberty too well to be in a hurry to give it up for any mortal man.'

'You think so now but there'll come a time when you'll love him tremendously and live and die for him. I know you will, it's your way and I shall have to stand by and see it,' said he, with an expression so very tragic!

'Yes, I will live and die for him, if he ever comes and makes me love him in spite of myself!' cried Jo. 'I shall always be fond of you, very fond indeed, as a friend but I'll never marry you!

The sooner you believe it the better for both of us!'

Laurie looked at her, saying in a desperate sort of tone, 'You'll be sorry some day, Jo.'

The next moment, Laurie swung down the bank toward the river but she knew that Laurie was not the weak sort who would give in by a single failure. He had no thought of a melodramatic plunge but some blind instinct led him to fling hat and coat into his boat and row away with all his might. Jo drew a long breath, as she watched the poor fellow trying to manage the trouble which he carried in his heart.

She went straight to Mr Laurence, told the hard story bravely and then broke down, crying so dismally that the kind old gentleman, though sorely disappointed, did not utter a reproach.

When Laurie came home, dead tired but quite composed, his grandfather met him as if he knew nothing and kept up the delusion very successfully for an hour or two. But when they sat together in the twilight, it was hard work for the old man to ramble on as if all was fine! Laurie bore it as long as he could, then went to his piano and began to play. The windows were open and Jo, walking in the garden with Beth, for once understood music better than her sister, for he played the 'Sonata Pathetique', and played it as he never did before.

'That's very fine, I dare say, but it's sad enough to make one cry. Give us something gay, lad,' said Mr Laurence, whose kind old heart was full of sympathy. Laurie dashed into a livelier strain, played stormily for several minutes and would have got through bravely, if he hadn't heard Mrs March calling, 'Jo, dear, come in. I want you.'

Just what Laurie longed to say, with a different meaning! As he listened, he lost his control and the music ended with a broken cord and the musician sat silent in the dark. The old gentleman could not bear it any further, he placed a kind hand on Laurie's broad shoulders, and said gently, 'I know, my boy, I know.'

Laurie did not answer for an instant then asked sharply, 'Who told you?'

'Jo!'

Mr Laurence with unusual mildness, spoke, 'You won't care to stay at home now, perhaps?'

'I don't intend to run away because of a girl. Jo can't prevent my seeing her and I shall stay and do it as long as I like,' replied Laurie in a defiant tone.

'Not if you are the gentleman I think you are. I'm disappointed but the girl can't help it and the only thing left for you to do is to go away for a while. Where would you like to go?'

'Anywhere. I don't care what becomes of me,' replied Laurie recklessly which troubled his grandfather.

'Bear it like a man and don't do anything rash, for God's sake. Why not go abroad? I shall go with you.'

'Well, sir, what is the plan?' and Laurie sat down, completely disinterested, while Mr Laurence narrated the plan.

'Just as you like, sir. It doesn't matter where I go or what I do,' said Laurie in a spiritless tone.

'It does to me, remember that, my lad. I give you entire liberty, but I trust you to make an honest use of it. Promise me that, Laurie.'

'Anything you like, sir.'

Mr Laurence was ready with all arrangements and before his grandson recovered spirit enough to rebel, they were off. When the parting came he got on very well till Mrs March kissed him, with a whisper full of motherly solicitude. Jo followed a minute later to say goodbye. He put his arms about her, looked up at her with a face that made his short appeal eloquent and pathetic.

'Oh, Jo, can't you?'

'Teddy, dear, I wish I could!'

Laurie straightened himself up, said, 'It's all right, never mind,' and went away without another word. She knew it wasn't all right and Jo felt as if she had stabbed her dearest friend.

### Chapter Highlights

- Laurie graduates with honours and everyone is proud of him.
- Laurie asks Jo to meet him the next day, something which Jo dreads. She remembers how she used to look forward to meeting him but now she wants to run away from him.
- While they are returning home, Laurie confesses his love for Jo. Jo says that the reason she went away was because of him.
- Jo says that she is very fond of him but she does not love him like he loves her. Laurie is disappointed but then comes to the conclusion that Jo is in love with the Professor she has told him about and is angry. Jo assures him that she is not in love with him and that he is a good friend.
- She goes on to say that she does not plan to marry but Laurie concludes that she will learn to love the Professor and he will have to stand by and see them so.
- Hurt, Laurie abruptly leaves her. Gathering all her courage, Jo goes to Laurie's grandfather and tells him everything that has happened. The old gentleman is disappointed but does not reproach her.
- Later, Mr Laurence suggests that Laurie should go away for a while. Laurie agrees and Mr Laurence makes all the arrangements before his grandson could protest.

## Chapter 21

When Jo came home that spring, she had been struck with the change in Beth. No one spoke of it or seemed aware of it, for it had come too gradually to startle those who saw her daily, but to eyes sharpened by absence, it was very plain and a heavy weight fell on Jo's heart as she saw her sister's face. It was paler and thinner. Jo felt it but said nothing. Beth appeared happy and soon, Jo forgot her fear.

After Laurie left, Jo showed her savings and proposed a mountain trip, Beth had thanked her heartily but suggested that a short trip to the seaside would suit her better. Jo took Beth down to the quiet place, where she could live much in the open air so that the fresh sea breeze could put some colour into her pale cheeks.

Jo felt as if a veil had fallen between her heart and Beth's, and she waited for Beth to speak. One day Beth spoke. She lay so still that Jo thought she was asleep. For a minute her eyes welled up and when they cleared, she found Beth looking up at her so tenderly that there was hardly any need for her to say, 'Jo, dear, I'm glad you know it. I've tried to tell you, but I couldn't.'

'I've known it for quite some time and now it isn't hard to bear it. Try to see it this way and don't be troubled about me, this is the best!'

'Is this that made you so unhappy in the autumn, Beth? You

have kept it to yourself so long, did you?' asked Jo.

'Yes, I gave up hoping then but I didn't want to admit it. When I saw you all so well and strong and full of happy plans, it was hard to believe that I could never be like you and was miserable. That is when you saw me weep, Jo.'

'Oh, Beth, you didn't let me comfort and help you? How could you shut me out and bear it all alone?' Jo's voice was full of tender reproach and her heart ached to think of Beth's solitary struggle as she learnt to say goodbye to health, love and life.

'It would have been selfish to frighten you all when Marmee was so anxious about Meg and Amy away and you so happy with Laurie, at least I thought so then.'

'And I thought you loved him, Beth, and I went away because I couldn't hurt you,' cried Jo, glad to blurt out the truth.

Beth looked so amazed at the idea that Jo smiled in spite of her pain and added softly, 'I was afraid that your little heart was full of lovelornity!'

'How could I, when he was so fond of you?' asked Beth, as innocently as a child. 'I love him but he could never be anything to me but my brother. I hope he truly will be, sometime.'

'Not through me,' said Jo decidedly. 'Amy is left for him and they would suit excellently! I don't care about anybody except you, Beth. You must get well! I can't let you go. I'll work and pray and fight against it. God won't be so cruel as to take you from me,' cried poor Jo rebelliously.

After a while, Beth asked, with recovered serenity, 'Will you tell them this when we go home?'

'I think they will see it without words,' sighed Jo, for now it seemed to her that Beth changed every day.

'If they don't see it, you will tell them for me. I don't want any secrets and it's kinder to prepare them.'

She was right. There was no need of any words when they

got home. Father and Mother saw what they had prayed to be saved from seeing. Tired with her short journey, Beth went to bed, saying how glad she was to be home and when Jo went down, she found her father stood leaning his head on the mantelpiece and did not turn as she came in but her mother stretched out her arms as if for help and Jo went to comfort her without a word.

### Chapter Highlights

- Ever since Jo had returned, she had seen that Beth is thinner and paler than usual. She is afraid but seeing that she is happy, she is at ease.
- After Laurie leaves, Jo suggests that Beth should go on a trip. Beth asks to go to the seaside with Jo. It is here that Beth finally reveals what has been troubling her.
- Beth says that she had known for a very long time that she will die soon and will not be able to see her family grow. She knows that Jo knows about it and confesses that she too wants a life like her sisters but will not have one.
- Jo confesses that she once thought that Beth loved Laurie. Beth smiles and says that she has always loved him as a brother.
- Beth asks Jo to tell everyone about her deteriorating health when they return home. It is time that they should prepare themselves. But as they return home, they find that Mr and Mrs March already knew and seeing Beth paler than ever, they knew they will lose their daughter.

# Chapter 22

At three o'clock in the afternoon, all the fashionable world at Nice is seen on the Promenade des Anglais, a charming place, for the wide walk, bordered with palms, flowers, and tropical shrubs, is bound on one side by the sea, on the other by the grand drive, lined with hotels and villas.

Along this walk, on Christmas Day, a tall young man walked slowly, with a somewhat absentminded expression. He looked like an Italian, was dressed like an Englishman and had the independent air of an American, a combination which caused sundry pairs of feminine eyes to look approvingly at him.

The young man took little notice of them, except to glance now and then at some blonde girl in blue.

Presently the quick trot of pony's feet made him look up, as one of the little carriages, with a single young lady, came rapidly down the street. The lady was young, blonde, and dressed in blue. He stared a minute, then his whole face lit up and waving his hat like a school boy, he hurried forward to meet her.

'Oh, Laurie, is it really you? I thought you'd never come!' cried Amy.

'I had promised to spend Christmas with you and here I am.'

'I have so much to say, I don't know where to begin! Get in and we shall talk at length. There is a Christmas party at our hotel. I am sure you'll come with us! Aunt will be charmed.'

'Thank you,' said Laurie, leaning back and folding his arms, allowing her to drive for that afforded her infinite satisfaction.

'Tell me all about yourself. The last I heard from your grandfather was that you were in Berlin.'

'I spent a month there and then joined him in Paris, where he has settled for the winter. He has friends there and finds plenty to amuse him and we get on capitally.'

'That's a sociable arrangement,' said Amy. While Laurie listlessly looked around, Amy watched him and felt a strange sort of shyness steal over her, for he had changed. He was no longer the merry-faced boy she remembered. He was handsomer than ever and greatly improved, she thought. He looked tired and spiritless, not exactly unhappy. She couldn't understand it but remained quiet.

'Beth is very unwell, Mother has written. I often think I ought to go home but they all say 'stay' for I shall never have another chance like this,' said Amy, looking sober over the letter.

'I think they are right! You are happy and enjoying so much, my dear.'

He looked more like his old self as he said that.

'This will truly be a merry Christmas to me, with presents in the morning, you in the afternoon, and a party at night,' said Amy, as they drove on.

While Amy laughed Laurie looked at her, with a natural curiosity to see what changes time had wrought. He found much to admire and approve, for overlooking a few little affectations of speech and manner, she was as sprightly and graceful as ever. Her strong will still held its own and her native frankness was unspoiled by foreign polish.

So after idling away an hour, they drove home again and having paid his respects to Mrs Carrol, Laurie left them, promising to return in the evening.

Amy deliberately worked hard on looking stunning that night. Time and absence had done its work on both the young people. She had seen her old friend in a new light, as a handsome and agreeable man. Amy knew her good points and made the most of them.

She looked unusually gay and graceful as she walked down the long saloon and waited for Laurie who came in so quietly that she did not hear him.

'Good evening, Diana!' said Laurie.

'Good evening, Apollo!' she answered, smiling back at him, for he too looked unusually debonair, and the thought of entering the ballroom on the arm of such a handsome man caused her heart to flutter.

The Christmas ball was a great hit. Before the evening was half over, Laurie had concluded that 'little Amy was going to make a very charming woman'.

Amy didn't understand why Laurie looked at her so kindly, and devoted himself to her for the rest of the evening but the impulse that wrought this agreeable change was the result of one of the new impressions which both of them were unconsciously giving and receiving.

### Chapter Highlights

- It is a pleasant day in Nice. Laurie is walking down an avenue with an absent-minded expression but his appearance is receiving a lot of attention from women.
- Suddenly, trot of a pony coming down the street catches his attention. He looks up and sees Amy in the carriage. He takes off his hat and greets her saying that he has kept his promise to spend Christmas with her.

- Together they go to a party where Amy is going to meet her aunt. Laurie tells him that he has been to Berlin and Paris before coming to Nice.
- Amy notices that he has somehow changed and is no longer the shy boy she knew earlier. Laurie too notices that Amy has become graceful and charming.
- She tells him that Beth's health has worsened and she wishes to go home but Marmee says that she will not get this chance again. They talk about many things until they decide to return home.
- After paying his respects to Aunt Carrol, Laurie leaves while Amy goes to dress for the party. Later, together, they go to the party. By the time the party ends, Laurie has concluded that Amy will make a very charming woman.

## Chapter 23

The most pleasant room of the house was set apart for Beth. It contained everything that she most loved—flowers, pictures, her piano, the little worktable and the beloved pussies. Father's best books found their way there, Mother's easy chair, Jo's desk and Amy's finest sketches. Everyday Meg brought her babies to amuse Aunt Beth. John quietly set apart a little sum, that he might keep the dainty darling supplied with the fruit she loved.

Old Hannah never wearied of concocting dainty dishes to tempt a hearty appetite, shedding tears as she worked. From across the sea came little gifts and cheerful letters.

The first few months were very happy ones. Beth would look around and say 'How beautiful this is!' as they all sat together in her sunny room.

This peaceful time was a preparation for the sad hours to come. After a while Beth grew so weak that talking tired her, pain overpowered her and her tranquil spirit was sorrowfully perturbed.

Jo never left her for an hour since Beth had said, 'I feel stronger when you are here.' It was here that Jo received lessons in patience, charity and forgiveness.

'Be kind to everyone. You must take my place, Jo and be everything to Father and Mother when I'm gone. They will turn to you, don't fail them!' she would tell Jo.

Spring came and went. The flowers were up fairly early and the birds returned as if to bid goodbye to Beth. With tears, prayers and tender hands, Mother and sisters made her ready for the long sleep that pain would never mar again, seeing the serenity that soon replaced the anguished body.

### Chapter Highlights

- After the initial shock, the family prepares a special room for Beth. All her favourite things are there. Meg brings her children to amuse her each day. Even Hannah prepares meals that Beth likes.
- After some months, Beth finds it difficult to talk for long and pain overpowers her at once. Little by little, the cheerful face loses its happiness.
- Jo stays by her side all this time. It is during this time that Jo learns to be patient and forgiving. Often Beth asks Jo to look after everyone when she is gone.
- When spring comes, the March family realizes that soon they must say goodbye to their beloved Beth.

## Chapter 24

Laurie thought that the task of forgetting his love for Jo would absorb all his powers for years but surprisingly he discovered it grew easier every day. He refused to believe it at first, got angry with himself and couldn't understand it. Laurie's heart healed with a rapidity that astonished him.

He wrote to Jo, telling her that he did not feel settled while there was the least hope of her changing her mind. Couldn't she, wouldn't she—and let him come home and be happy? He waited with feverish impatience for an answer. It finally came and settled his mind for Jo decidedly couldn't and wouldn't. She was wrapped up in Beth and never wished to hear about it again.

Then she begged him to be happy with somebody else but always keep a little corner of his heart for his loving sister Jo. In a postscript she requested him not to tell Amy that Beth was worse; she was coming home in the spring and there was no need of saddening the remainder of her stay.

'So I will, at once. Poor little girl, it will be a sad going home for her, I'm afraid,' and Laurie wrote to her on his best paper.

The letter was promptly answered, for Amy was homesick. The correspondence flourished famously and letters flew to and fro between Laurie and Amy with unfailing regularity all through the early spring.

Amy asked his opinion on all subjects; she was interested in everything he did, made charming little presents for him, and sent him two letters a week! She sat for hours on the terrace at Valrosa, lost in thoughts.

Amy was very homesick but she bore it bravely and quietly agreed to the family decree that she should not shorten her visit. However, she longed to be at home. Every day she sat looking wistfully across the lake, waiting for Laurie to come and comfort her. The moment Laurie received the letter about Beth's death, he packed his knapsack and was off to keep his promise. He knew Vevay well and he knew that Amy might be in the chateau garden.

In the pleasant old garden on the borders of the lovely lake, he found her sitting on a bench. Leaning her head on her hand, with a homesick heart and heavy eyes, she was thinking of Beth and wondering why Laurie did not come. She did not hear him walk up. He stood a minute, seeing what no one had ever seen before, the tender side of Amy's character. The minute she saw him, dropping everything, she ran to him, exclaiming in a tone of unmistakable love and longing, 'Oh, Laurie, I knew you'd come to me!'

I think everything was said and settled then, for as they stood together quite silent for a moment, with the dark head bent down protectively over the light one, Amy felt that no one could comfort and sustain her better than Laurie. He too decided that Amy was the only woman in the world who could fill Jo's place and make him happy.

'I came the minute I heard. I wish I could say something to comfort you for the loss of dear little Beth, but I can only feel!'

'I dread returning to a home without Beth much as I long to be with them all!'

'Poor little soul, you look as if you'd grieved yourself half sick! I'm going to take care of you, so don't cry any more. '

He felt more at ease and Amy found it pleasant to have a

strong arm to lean upon, a familiar face to smile at her, and a kind voice to talk delightfully to her alone. For an hour this new pair walked and talked and when dinner was announced, Mrs Carrol saw the girl's altered face, she exclaimed to herself, 'Now I understand! She has been pining for young Laurence. Bless my heart, I never thought of such a thing!' That good lady, then, invited Laurie to stay with them.

In spite of the new sorrow, it was a very happy time. There was no need of telling Amy that he loved her, she knew it without words. Laurie let the days pass, and leaving his proposal, to chance. It, however, came on the lake at noonday in a few blunt words.

Laurie was leaning on his oars when Amy said hastily, 'You must be tired. Let me row. It will do me good.'

'I'm not tired but you may take an oar, if you like. Amy accepted an oar and rowed well, using both hands, unlike Laurie.

'How well we pull together, don't we?' said Amy.

'So well that I wish we might always pull in the same boat. Will you, Amy?' he asked very tenderly.

'Yes, Laurie,' she replied, very demurely.

They stopped rowing and very spontaneously added a pretty little tableau of human love and happiness to the dissolving views reflected in the lake.

## Chapter Highlights

- Laurie's love for Jo meanwhile diminishes by degree. He is unable to understand why this is happening and is angry.
- In his confusion, he writes to Jo asking her to consider his proposal again but Jo would not. In her reply, she tells him that he will be happy with someone else but he must keep a corner of his heart for his sister Jo. She also writes to him about Beth's declining health but begs him not to tell Amy about it and end her happiness before she returns home.
- Amy, however, is terribly homesick and wants to return home. At the same time, a good deal of letters are exchanged between Laurie and Amy and they have become fond of each other.
- Meanwhile, news comes of Beth's passing. No sooner does Laurie learn of it that he rushes to meet Amy to comfort her. He finds her in her aunt's house looking into the distance thinking about Beth. As he comforts her for her loss they both realize that they can stay together.
- Amidst this sorrowful time, Laurie's proposal to Amy is the reason to celebrate.

# Chapter 25

It was easy to make promises to Beth but when only loneliness and grief remained, Jo found it hard to keep her promise. How could she comfort Father and Mother when her own heart ached with a ceaseless longing for her sister, how could she make the house cheerful when all its light, warmth and beauty seemed to have deserted it. They were dark and trying days for poor Jo!

Often while sleeping, when the sight of the little empty bed made her cry, Marmee came to comfort her, not only with words but the patient tenderness that soothes by a touch, tears that were mute reminders of a greater grief than Jo's. One day, she went to her father and said, 'Father, talk to me as you did to Beth.'

'My dear, nothing can comfort me like this,' he answered, with a falter in his voice, and both arms round her, as if he too, needed help and did not fear to ask for it.

The parents who had taught one child to meet death without fear, were teaching another to accept life without despondency or distrust and to use its beautiful opportunities with gratitude and power.

Jo discovered, as she sat with Meg, sewing together, how much her sister had improved. 'Marriage is an excellent thing, after all. I wonder if I should blossom out half as well as you have,' said Jo, as she constructed a kite for Demi.

'It's just what you need to bring out the tender womanly half of your nature, Jo. You are like a chestnut burr, prickly outside, but silky-soft within and a sweet kernel, if one can only get at it. Love will make you show your heart one day, and then the rough burr will fall off.'

'Why don't you resume writing? That always made you happy,' said her mother once, when Jo was overpowered by despondency.

'I've no heart to write and even if I did, nobody likes to read what I write.'

'We do. Write something for us and never mind the rest of the world. Try it, dear. I'm sure it would do you good and please us very much,' added her father.

But despite her doubts, Jo wrote. Jo never knew how it happened but something got into that story that went straight to the hearts of those who read it.

When her family had laughed and cried over it, her father sent it, much against her will, to one of the popular magazines and to her utter surprise, it was not only paid for, but requests for more poured in.

Strangers as well as friends admired it.

'I don't understand it. What's there in a simple little story like that to make people praise it so?' said Jo, quite bewildered.

'There is truth in it, Jo, that's the secret. Humour and pathos make it alive, and you have found your style at last. You wrote with no thoughts of fame and money and put your heart into it.'

After a while, when Amy and Laurie wrote of their engagement, Mrs March feared that Jo wouldn't be able to rejoice over it but her fears were soon set to rest, for though Jo looked grave at first, she took it quietly and was full of hopes and plans for the two.

'My dear, I fancied it would upset you to learn that your Teddy loved someone else.'

'Mother, could I be so silly and selfish, after I'd refused his love?'

'I knew you were sincere then, Jo, but lately I have thought that if he came back and asked you again, you might perhaps, give him another answer. Forgive me, dear, I can't help seeing that you are very lonely. So I fancied that your Teddy might fill the empty place if he tried now.'

'No, Mother, it is better as it is. I'm glad Amy has learnt to love him but you are right in one thing. I am lonely and if Teddy had tried again, I might have said "Yes", not because I love him but because I need to be loved more than when he went away.'

'I'm glad, Jo, for it shows that you are getting on. There are plenty to love you, till the best lover of all comes to give you your reward.'

After a while, Jo roamed away upstairs, a restless spirit possessed her, not bitter as it once was, but a patient wonder why one sister should have all she asked, the other nothing. Up in the garret, stood four little wooden chests in a row, each marked with its owner's name and filled with relics of childhood and girlhood. Jo stared at an old exercise book that took her back to that pleasant winter at Mrs Kirke's. She smiled when she came to a little message written in the Professor's hand, 'Wait for me, my friend. I may be a little late, but I shall surely come.'

Her lips began to tremble, as the friendly words took a new meaning and touched a tender spot in her heart.

'It would be wonderful if he comes! So kind, so good, so patient with me always, my dear old Fritz. I didn't value him enough when I had him but now how I should love to see him! I'm so lonely!'

## Chapter Highlights

- After Beth's death, Jo finds it difficult to comfort anyone and make the house cheerful once more. She misses her sister desperately. Often, seeing Beth's empty bed makes her cry. Even Mr and Mrs March find it difficult to hide their tears.
- Jo spends time with Meg sewing to stop being sorrowful. One day, her parents ask her to begin writing once more for them.
- Despite her doubts, Jo writes. Something about the story touches everyone's hearts. Then, her father sends her story to one of the popular magazines and to her surprise she is not only paid for it but asked to write more of the kind.
- Jo wonders why everyone is praising her story so much. Her mother says that it is because she has put all her heart into it and told the truth.
- Soon, Laurie and Amy announce their engagement. Jo is uncertain at first hearing about it but soon she is busy making plans for the two. However, both Mrs March and her realize that she is lonely.
- While wandering in the house by herself, Jo comes across one of her old notebooks and finds a note for from Professor Bhaer where he had written that he will come to see her. Jo, wholeheartedly wishes that he does come for she is very lonely.

## Chapter 26

Jo lay on the sofa, thinking. She used to lie there on Beth's little red pillow, planning stories, dreaming or remembering her dear sister who never seemed far away. Jo was sad, for the next day was her birthday. She was thinking how fast the years went by and how little she seemed to have accomplished.

Jo must have fallen asleep for suddenly Laurie's ghost seemed to lean over her. She lay staring at him in startled silence, till he stooped and kissed her. Then she knew that she wasn't dreaming and flew up, crying joyfully, 'Oh my Teddy!'

'So you are glad to see me?'

'Glad! Words can't express my happiness! Where's Amy?'

'Your mother has got her down at Meg's. We stopped there by the way and there was no getting my wife out of their clutches.'

'Your what? So you've already got married!' cried Jo.

'Very much so, thank you.'

'You take one's breath away, creeping in like a burglar and letting cats out of bags like that? Tell me all about it, Teddy!'

'How good it's to hear you say 'Teddy'! No one ever calls me that but you,' replied Laurie, as he sat down with an air of great contentment.

Laurie narrated the facts so freely and so naturally that she was assured that Laurie had forgiven and forgotten. She tried to draw away her hand but Laurie held it fast, and said, 'Jo, dear, I want to say one thing that I never shall stop loving you, but the love is altered. Amy and you changed places in my heart, that's all. You both got into your right places and I could honestly share my heart between sister Jo and wife Amy and love them dearly.'

'This last year has been really hard, Jo and we left you to bear it alone, while we were enjoying. Your eyes look sad and when I touched the cushion, I found it wet! What a selfish beast I've been!' added Laurie, with the most remorseful look.

Jo turned over the pillow and answered, forcing a cheerful tone, 'No, I had Father and Mother to help me, the dear babies to comfort me and the thought that you and Amy were safe and happy. I am lonely, sometimes, but I guess it's good for me!'

'You shall never again be lonely,' broke in Laurie. 'Amy and I can't get on without you.'

'I begin to feel quite happy already, Teddy,' and Jo leaned her head on his shoulder.

In trooped the whole family. Everyone was hugged and kissed over and over again. Finally, the three wanderers were allowed to sit and exulted over. Mr Laurence, hale and hearty as ever, had improved by his foreign tour.

Jo thought, as she watched the pair, 'How well they look together! I was right! Laurie has found the beautiful, accomplished girl who will become his home better than the clumsy Jo, be a pride, not a torment to him.' Mrs March and her husband smiled and nodded at each other with happy faces, for they were satisfied to see their youngest had done well.

Such a happy procession moved into the little dining room! Mr March proudly escorted Mrs Laurence. Mrs March proudly leaned on the arm of 'my son'. The old gentleman took Jo, with a whispered, 'You must be my girl now,' that made Jo whisper back, 'I'll try to fill her place, sir.'

A sudden sense of loneliness came over her so strongly that

she had tears in her eyes, for even Teddy had deserted her. Just then, she heard a knock at the porch door. She opened with hospitable haste and was startled as if another ghost had come to surprise her, for there stood a tall bearded gentleman, beaming at her.

'Oh, Mr Bhaer, I am so glad to see you!' cried Jo, hugging him.

'Miss March, even I am most delighted but I see you have a party,' and the professor paused as the sound of voices came down to him.

'No, it's just the family. My sister and friends have just come home and we are all very happy. Please join us.'

'I shall gladly meet the family! Have you been ill, my friend?'

'Not ill but tired and sorrow-stricken. We have had trouble since I saw you last.'

'Ah, yes, I know. My heart was sore for you when I heard that,' and he shook hands so warmly that Jo felt as if no comfort could equal the look of the kind eyes, the grasp of the big, warm hand.

'Father, Mother, this is my friend, Professor Bhaer,' she said, with a face and a tone of irrepressible pride and pleasure.

If the stranger had any doubts about his reception, they were soon put to rest, for everyone warmed upto him almost immediately.

Laurie, stood aloof at first, observing the newcomer with brotherly circumspection. Soon, he got interested in spite of himself and before he knew it, was drawn into the circle. Mr Bhaer seldom spoke to Laurie, but he looked at him often and a shadow would pass across his face, as he watched the young man in his prime. Then his eyes would wistfully turn to Jo.

Jo cast a stealthy glance now and then. Mr Bhaer looked all alive with interest in the present moment, actually young and handsome, she thought, forgetting to compare him with Laurie. Jo glowed with triumph when Teddy got into a discussion with him. Nobody knew where the evening went to, for Hannah had skilfully taken the babies at an early hour and put them to bed. Mr Laurence went home to rest. The others sat round the fire, talking away, utterly regardless of the lapse of time.

After a while, the professor said, 'I too shall take everyone's leave but I shall gladly come again, dear madam, for a little business in the city will keep me here some days.'

He spoke to Mrs March but he looked at Jo, and the mother's voice gave as cordial an assent as did the daughter's eyes, for Mrs March was not blind to her children's interest.

'That is a wise man,' remarked Mr March, with placid satisfaction.

'I know he is a good one,' added Mrs March, with decided approval.

### Chapter Highlights

- One day, Jo is lying on Beth's bed and thinking. She must have fallen asleep when suddenly it seems to her that Laurie is standing near her.
- A moment later, she realizes that it is Laurie and greets him enthusiastically. Laurie tells her that he and Amy are married and that her mother had taken her to Meg's.
- Quickly, he tells her how it came about and then looking at Jo, he says that she and Amy have fallen into the right places in his heart and that he is never going to stop loving his sister Jo and wife Amy.
- Laurie continues, saying that while everyone had a good time, she was left to deal with the hard times alone. Jo smiles and says that she has had her parents with her and the babies to comfort her but that she feels lonely.

- Later, at the dinner table, everyone is happy. As Mr Laurence leads Jo to the dining table, he asks her to take the place of Beth in his life. Jo says she will try but this brings tears to her eyes and a great sense of loneliness engulfs her.
- Just then, there is a knock on the front door. Jo opens the door and is surprised. Professor Bhaer is standing, beaming at her. She ushers him in. He apologizes for coming at a time when the family is celebrating. However, he notices that her eyes are sad. Minutes later, everyone is welcoming him warmly. Laurie, however, looks at him carefully before he too starts to like him.
- The evening becomes memorable. Meg leaves with the babies in time and Mr Laurence too leaves to rest.
- After a while, when Professor Bhaer took his leave, he mentions that he going to stay in the town for some time. After his departure, Mr and Mrs March, silently approve Jo's choice.

## Chapter 27

While Laurie and Amy were planning a blissful future, Mr Bhaer and Jo were enjoying promenades of a different sort, along muddy roads and sodden fields.

'I always walk in the evening so why I should give it up, just because I happen to meet the Professor on the way,' said Jo to herself, after two or three encounters.

By the second week, everyone knew perfectly well what was going on, yet they pretended to be blind to the changes in Jo's face and behaviour. They never asked why she sang about her work, did her hair three times a day and why she looked so radiant after her evening walk.

Jo was afraid of being laughed at for surrendering, after her vehement declarations of independence. Laurie was her especial dread, but thanks to the new manager, Amy, he behaved with praiseworthy propriety. Yet he exulted in private and longed for the time when he could tease her.

The Professor came and went with lover-like regularity for a fortnight. Then he stayed away for three whole days without any indication. This caused everybody to look sober and Jo to become pensive, at first and then, angry.

'It's disgusting! He's gone home as suddenly as he came. Though it doesn't matter to me but he should have said goodbye to us like a gentleman,' she mumbled to herself, as she put on her things for the customary walk one dull afternoon.

'You'd better carry your umbrella, dear. It looks like rain,' said her mother as Jo was about to step out.

'Yes, Marmee, do you want anything from the town? I've got to get some paper,' returned Jo.

Quickly, Marmee told her what she wanted.

'If you happen to meet Mr Bhaer, bring him home to tea. I quite long to see the dear man,' added Mrs March.

Jo heard that but did not reply, except to kiss her mother and walk rapidly away.

Jo walked into the town for a long time, thinking, when it started to drizzle. Then, Jo realized that she had forgotten her umbrella.

Jo hurried on, with increasing dampness about the ankles and much clashing of umbrellas overhead. The fact that a somewhat dilapidated blue one remained stationary above the unprotected bonnet, attracted her attention and looking up, she saw Mr Bhaer looking down.

'I wish to know from the strong-minded lady who goes so bravely under many horse noses and so fast through much mud, what brought her here?'

'I'm shopping.'

Mr Bhaer smiled, but he only said, 'You have no umbrella. May I come along and carry your bundles?'

'Yes, thank you.'

Jo's cheeks were as red as her ribbon and she wondered what he thought of her, but she didn't care, for in a minute she found herself walking away arm in arm with her professor, feeling as if the sun had suddenly burst out with uncommon brilliance, that the world was all right again!

'We thought you had gone,' said Jo hastily.

'Could I have left without a farewell to those who have been so heavenly kind to me?' he asked so reproachfully that she felt as if she had insulted him and answered heartily, 'No, I didn't but we rather missed you, Father and Mother especially.'

'And you?'

'I'm always glad to see you, sir.' This was spoken in such a frosty tone that the professor's smile vanished, as he said gravely, 'I shall come one more time before I leave.'

'You are going, then?'

'I have no longer any business here, it is done. My friends found for me a place in a college, where I will teach and earn enough to make a living.'

'How splendid it will be to have you doing what you like and be able to see you and the boys often!' cried Jo, unable to conceal her excitement and joy!

'We shall not meet often, I fear, this place is far from here, on the western side!'

'So far away!' she replied, disappointed. Mr Bhaer could read several languages but he did not understand women yet. He thought that he knew Jo pretty well and was, therefore, confused by the contradictions of voice, face and manner, which unravelled before him in rapid succession that day, for she was in half a dozen different moods in the course of half an hour.

'I need to buy a few things from here! Will you come in? It won't take long.'

When they came out, he put the parcel under his arm with a more cheerful aspect and, together they splashed through the puddles, enjoying themselves thoroughly.

'Should we shop a little for the babies and have a farewell feast tonight if I go for my last call at your pleasant home?' he asked, stopping before a window full of fruit and flowers.

The two shopped and came out with their hands full. He put the packets in his large pockets, gave her the flowers to hold and holding the old umbrella, over their heads, they walked on again.

'Shall we go home?' he asked.

'Yes, it's late and I'm so tired.' Jo's voice was sad for she had expected him to make some sort of a proposal and the sun seemed to have gone in as suddenly as it came out. The world grew muddy and miserable again. For the first time she discovered that her feet were cold, her head ached, and that her heart was full of pain. Mr Bhaer was going away; he only cared for her as a friend.

Mr Bhaer saw the tears on her cheeks. The sight seemed to touch him very much, for suddenly stooping down, he asked in a tone that meant a great deal, 'Heart's dearest, why do you cry?'

Jo being new to this emotion replied, 'Because you are going away,' with an irrepressible sob.

'Ach, mein Gott, that is so good!' cried Mr Bhaer.

'Jo, I have nothing but much love to give you. I came to see if you could care for it and I wanted to be sure that I was more than a friend. Am I?' he added, all in one breath.

'Oh, yes!' said Jo with an expression that plainly showed how happy she would be to walk through life beside him.

It was certainly proposing under difficulties, for even if he had desired to do so, Mr Bhaer could not go down upon his knees, on account of the mud.

Neither could he offer Jo his hand, for both were full. So the only way in which he could express his rapture was to look at her with complete adoration.

'Now tell me what brought you here, exactly when I wanted you?' asked Jo.

'A poem called, 'IN THE GARRET'. I found it by chance and knew it by the names and the initials and in it there was one little verse that seemed to call me,' replied the professor.

'It's not very well written but I felt it when I wrote it, one day when I was very lonely. I never thought it would go and tell tales,' said Jo.

'I read that and realized that you were sad and lonely!' he answered.

'So you came and found that it was the one precious thing I needed,' whispered Jo.

'I had no courage to think that at first, heavenly kind as was your welcome to me. But soon I said to myself, "I will have her if I die for it!" cried Mr Bhaer.

'Have you the patience to wait a long time, Jo? I must go and do my work alone. Can you forgive that and be happy while we hope and wait?'

'Yes, I can, for we love each other and that makes all the rest easy to bear. I have my duty also and my work. So there's no need of hurry or impatience.'

### Chapter Highlights

- Over the next few days, Jo's behaviour changes. She is happy especially after coming back from her evening walks where she often meets the Professor.
- Everyone knows what is going on but they do not talk about it except Laurie who is waiting for a chance to tease Jo who loved her independence.
- After a fortnight of regular meetings, suddenly the Professor does not come for three days and Jo is angry.
- One evening, she goes to town to do some errands and forgets to take an umbrella and it starts to drizzle.
- Suddenly, she meets Professor Bhaer and they start walking together. She reproaches him for not coming and letting them think that he had returned. She mentions that

her parents missed him and so did she.

- The Professor says that he is going to leave soon and that if it is not much trouble, he can return with her to meet her family one last time. Jo is sad and the professor is unable to understand what is upsetting Jo.
- Suddenly, Jo has tears in her eyes. The Professor sees them and asks what is causing them. When Jo replies that it is because he is going away that the two end up confessing their love for each other. They, however, decide to wait and raise money for their home before settling down.

## Chapter 28

For a year Jo and her Professor worked and waited, hoped and loved, met occasionally and wrote voluminous letters. The second year began rather soberly, for their prospects did not brighten, and Aunt March died suddenly. However, when their first sorrow was over, they found they had a cause for rejoicing. She had left Plumfield to Jo, which made all sorts of joyful things possible.

'It's a fine old place and will bring a handsome sum, for of course if you intend to sell it,' said Laurie, as they were all talking the matter over some weeks later.

'No, I don't,' was Jo's decided answer.

'You don't mean to live there?'

'Yes, I do.'

'But, my dear girl, it's an immense house and will take large amounts of money to keep it in order. The garden and orchard alone need two or three men, and farming isn't in Bhaer's line!'

'He'll try his hand at it there, if I propose it. The crop we are going to raise is a profitable one,' and Jo laughed.

'Of what is this fine crop to consist, ma'am?'

'Boys. I want to open a school for little boys, a good, happy, homelike school, with me to take care of them and Fritz to teach them.'

'That's a truly "Joian" plan!' cried Laurie, to the family, who looked as much surprised as he.

'I like it,' said Mrs March decidedly.

'So do I,' added her husband.

'I knew you'd stand by me, sir. Amy does too—I see it in her eyes, though she prudently waits to turn it over in her mind before she speaks. My dear folks,' continued Jo earnestly, 'just understand that this is a long cherished plan. Before Fritz came, I intended to hire a big house, pick up some poor, forlorn little lads who hadn't any mothers, take care of them and make life jolly for them. I see so many going to ruin for want of help at the right minute; I love to do anything for them. I can feel their wants and would be a mother to them!'

'I told my plan to Fritz once and he said it was just what he would like. We agreed to try it when we got a little rich. Bless his dear heart, he's been doing it all his life, helping poor boys. I know he will never be rich. Money doesn't stay in his pocket long but now thanks to my good old aunt, who loved me better than I ever deserved, I'm rich, at least I feel so, and we can live at Plumfield perfectly well, if we have a flourishing school.

'It's just the place for boys, the house is big and the furniture strong and plain. I can feed, nurse, pet and scold them and Mother will be at my side. I will not go away from Marmee and Father.'

'May I enquire how you intend to support the establishment?' asked Laurie.

'Now don't be a wet-blanket, Teddy. Of course I shall have rich pupils, also—perhaps begin with such altogether. Then, when I've got a start, I can take in a ragamuffin or two, just for a relish. Rich people's children also need care and comfort! Besides, I've had experience, too, for haven't I brought up one boy to be the pride and honour to his family?'

'I'll testify that you did,' said Laurie with a grateful look.

'I am proud of you, Teddy, for you get better every year and everyone feels it.'

Poor Laurie didn't know where to look, for, man though he was, something of the old bashfulness came over him as this burst of praise made all faces turn approvingly upon him.

'I say, Jo, that's rather too much,' he began, just in his old boyish way. 'You have all done more for me than I can ever thank you for, except by doing my best not to disappoint you.'

That night when she went to her room, Jo sat beside her sister's bed and thought tenderly of Beth. It was an eventful year altogether, for things seemed to happen in an unusually rapid and delightful manner. Jo was married and settled at Plumfield. Then a family of six or seven boys sprung up like mushrooms and flourished surprisingly, poor boys as well as rich, for Mr Laurence was continually finding some touching case of destitution and begging the Bhaers to take pity on the child and he would gladly pay a trifle for its support. In this way, the sly old gentleman got round proud Jo and furnished her with the style of boy in which she most delighted.

It was an uphill task and Jo made mistakes but the wise Professor steered her safely into calmer waters and the wildest ragamuffin was conquered in the end. It became a sort of boys' paradise and Laurie suggested that it should be called 'Bhaer-garten', as a compliment to its master and appropriate to its inhabitants. It never was a fashionable school and the Professor did not lay up a fortune but it was just what Jo intended it to be: 'A happy, homelike place for boys, who needed teaching, care and kindness'.

Every room in the big house was soon full. Yes, Jo was a very happy woman there, in spite of hard work, much anxiety, and a perpetual racket. She enjoyed it heartily and found the applause of her boys more satisfying than any praise of the world. As the years went on, two little lads of her own came to increase her happiness, Rob, named for Grandpa and Teddy, a happy-go-lucky baby, who seemed to have inherited his papa's sunshiny temper as well as his mother's lively spirit. How they ever grew up in that whirlpool of boys was a mystery to their grandma and aunts!

There were a great many holidays at Plumfield, and one of the most delightful was the yearly apple-picking. The Marches, Laurences, Brookes and Bhaers turned out in full force. Five years after Jo's wedding, one of these festivals occurred, on a mellow October day, when the air was full of an exhilarating freshness. The old orchard wore its holiday attire. Birds twittered their adieux and every tree stood ready to send down its shower of red or yellow apples at the first shake. All declared that there never had been such a perfect day or such jolly set to enjoy it.

The Professor charged up and down the orchard with a pole, leading the boys. Laurie devoted himself to the little ones, rode his small daughter in a bushel-basket, took Daisy up among the bird's nests and prevented adventurous Rob from breaking his neck. Mrs March and Meg sat among the apple piles, sorting the contributions that kept pouring in, while Amy sketched the various groups.

Jo was in her element that day. She rushed about, her baby tucked under her arm, ready for any adventure which might turn up. Little Teddy bore a charmed life, for nothing ever happened to him and Jo was never worried about him.

At four o'clock, Jo and Meg, with help from the bigger boys, set forth the supper on the grass. When no one could eat any more, the professor proposed the first regular toast, which was always drunk at such times, 'Aunt March, God bless her!' She was never forgotten for the professor and Jo were truly grateful to her!

During the ceremony the boys had mysteriously disappeared and then, the professor suddenly began to sing. Then, from above him, voice after voice took up the words, and from tree to tree echoed the music of the unseen choir, as the boys sang with all their hearts the little song that Jo had written, Laurie set to music and the professor trained his lads to give with the best effect. This was something altogether new, and it proved a grand success. After this, the boys dispersed, leaving Mrs March and her daughters sitting and talking under the tree.

'I don't think I shall ever call myself "unlucky Jo" again, when my greatest wish has been so beautifully gratified,' said Mrs Bhaer.

As Amy sat quietly, a great tear dropped on the golden hair of the sleeping child in her arms, for her one well-beloved daughter was a frail little creature and the dread of losing her was the shadow over Amy's sunshine. Amy's nature was growing sweeter. Laurie was growing more serious and firm. Both were learning that beauty, youth, good fortune, even love, cannot keep care and pain, loss and sorrow, from the most blessed!

'There's no need for me to say it, for everyone can see that I'm far happier than I deserve,' added Jo, glancing from her good husband to her chubby children, tumbling on the grass beside her.

'Yes, Jo, I think your harvest will be a good one,' began Mrs March.

'Not half so good as yours, Mother. We never can thank you enough for the patient sowing and reaping you have done,' cried Jo, with the loving impetuosity which she never would outgrow.

Touched to the heart, Mrs March could only stretch out her arms, as if to gather her children and grandchildren to herself, and say, with face and voice full of motherly love, gratitude and humility, 'Oh, my girls, however long you may live, I never can wish you a greater happiness than this!'

## Chapter Highlights

- A year goes by when the Professor and Jo work and wait, hope and love and write letters to each other.
- . Suddenly, Aunt March dies leaving Jo her house.
- Jo decides to keep the house and turn a part of it into a school for boys. Everyone is surprised but they approve of the idea.
- She tells everyone that this is one of her plans which she wants to turn to reality. Professor Bhaer, or Fritz, too approves of it and the fact that he has been teaching boys all his life makes her plan perfect.
- Soon, Jo and the Professor marry and move into her aunt's house. In no time, the establishment becomes a school and rich as well as poor boys are being taught by Fritz. Mr Laurence helps them in their endeavour and is proud of Jo.
- In time, Jo and the professor have two boys of their own.
- Five years pass by since Jo's marriage. The time of apple picking is the most enjoyable time of the year and everyone joins in. After one such memorable day of apple-picking, Mrs March is sitting with her daughters and together they remember all the good times they had spent together and even then did not forgot those who had left them.

# Questions

### Chapter 1

1. Whom do the girls miss on Christmas?
2. Name the four March girls.
3. What surprise does their mother bring for the girls?

### Chapter 2

1. Who is Hannah?
2. What does Mother ask the girls to sacrifice?
3. What surprise comes for the girls on Christmas?

### Chapter 3

1. Where do Meg and Jo go?
2. Who does Jo meet at the dance?
3. What happens to Meg at the dance?

### Chapter 4

1. Why does Jo think that Laurie is lonely?
2. What is Jo's experience of being in Laurie's house?
3. Who is the old gentleman? What does Jo tell him about Laurie?

### Chapter 5

1. Who loves to play music?

2. What does Mr Laurence ask Beth to do?
3. What present does Beth get?

**Chapter 6**

1. Where do Meg and Jo go with Laurie?
2. Why is Amy angry? What does she do to take revenge?
3. How does Jo forgive Amy?

**Chapter 7**

1. Why did Jo go to the town?
2. Who does Jo meet in the town?
3. What is Jo's surprise?

**Chapter 8**

1. Where does Marmee has to go at once?
2. Who accompanies her on her journey?
3. Why does Marmee say that everyone is kind to them?

**Chapter 9**

3. Where did Beth go?
4. Where does Jo find her? How is she doing?
5. The March household is filled with sadness. How?

**Chapter 10**

1. Whose arrival makes everyone hopeful?
2. What does Jo suspect about Meg?
3. What does Mrs March think about John Brooke?

**Chapter 11**

1. What surprise is in store for Beth?
2. Who comes on Christmas?
3. How does the March family spend their evening?

## Chapter 12

1. How does Jo prepare Meg to face John Brooke?
2. Who comes unexpectedly and insults Mr Brooke?
3. What did the little confrontation leads to?

## Chapter 13

1. What changes take place in the March family?
2. What position does John take up?
3. What is the name of his and Meg's house?

## Chapter 14

1. Describe the preparations for the wedding day.
2. Who is considered 'the flower of the family'?
3. What does Laurie suggest to do at the party?

## Chapter 15

1. How does Jo's fortune take a turn?
2. What secret does Jo keep for six weeks?
3. What reward does she get?

## Chapter 16

1. Why does Laurie sneak into Meg's house?
2. What surprise does he get?
3. What are the names of Meg's twins?

## Chapter 17

1. Whom do Jo and Amy visit? What does Amy warn Jo about?
2. What surprise awaits Amy?
3. Why is Jo heartbroken?

**Chapter 18**

1. Why is Mrs March worried about Beth?
2. What does Jo suspect?
3. Where does Jo decide to go and why?

**Chapter 19**

1. What does Mr Dashwood observe about Jo?
2. What does he ask Jo to do?
3. Who is Professor Bhaer? Why does he disapprove of sensational stories?

**Chapter 20**

1. Why does Jo keep away from Laurie?
2. What does Jo goes to tell Mr Laurence?
3. What does Mr Laurence suggest Laurie to do?

**Chapter 21**

1. Where does Jo take Beth?
2. What is Beth's secret?
3. What does Beth ask Jo to do when they return home?

**Chapter 22**

1. Who meet in Nice?
2. How do Amy and Laurie's attitude towards each other change?
3. Where do they go together?

**Chapter 23**

1. How is everything made special for Beth?
2. What things amuse Beth?
3. How does her health deteriorate?

### Chapter 24

1. Why is Laurie confused?
2. What news fills everyone with sadness?
3. What news is the only ray of happiness?

### Chapter 25

1. How does Jo feel?
2. What does her parents encourage Jo to do?
3. Whom does Jo wants to come?

### Chapter 26

1. What surprise do Laurie and Amy bring?
2. Who comes on Christmas day?
3. How is Jo happy?

### Chapter 27

1. How has Jo changed?
2. Why had the Professor come to meet Jo?
3. How does the chapter end on a happy note?

### Chapter 28

1. What does Aunt March leave for Jo?
2. How does Jo and the Professor fulfil her dream?
3. What new festival are the Marches celebrating?